KALEIDOSCOPE

Imelda Megannety

KALEIDOSCOPE

To Narelle McGrath, Aidan Savage,

Stephen Keague, Tom Murphy,

My wonderful daughter-in-law,

and Sons-in-law

For their practical help, support and

Encouragement.

Cover from oil painting by Marie-Claire Keague

Copyright ©2019 Imelda Megannety
All rights reserved
ISBN 9781711169194

Chapter 1

In her late teenage years, Marianne was asked what her childhood had been like. She replied 'Normal, I suppose.' Only much later would it sink in that her family life had not been normal. She knew that she loved going to her friends' homes for play dates or parties and her brother Mark did too. She enjoyed the freedom and atmosphere she encountered there and thought it all wonderful if a bit strange. They did not have many children visiting their home. Usually there was a reason for this; Mum might not be well or just too busy; Dad might be working in his office at home and the noise of the children would disturb him. Playing outside in the garden was alright so long as there was no shouting or unruliness. Their parents preferred them to play quietly in their bedrooms or watch television. They had desks in their bedrooms and were expected to do their homework and study or read there. Mealtimes were very regimented and timewise, the same every day. The fact that their parents seldom communicated, had gradually grown into normality for the children, they were used to seeing notes on the kitchen worktop written by either parent, to the other, or else they got verbal messages from one parent to give the other.

Marianne's mother was a research secretary once, until she, Marianne, was about three years of age. Then she became a full-time mother and housewife. Her father was a psychiatrist at the nearby hospital. He also had a private clinic in the city. They both enjoyed the respect of the community and were very generous in their contributions to community causes, like the school library, the football pitch and educational toys to the local creche. Nobody could fault them on their attendance at any communal event or school play or sports day. They were widely regarded as 'pillars' of the community. They occupied the top pew every Sunday in the parish church.

Their house was in a good area, well maintained but not ostentatious. Both parents drove normal family cars and the children had bicycles which they rode to school. Their clothes never screamed 'expensive', there were no designer labels in their modest wardrobes.

They were well integrated children, popular with their peers and interested in everything around them. Their teachers always spoke highly of them and admired their achievements even if they were not highly academic. Their school reports were above average because they were such well-behaved and liked pupils. As Marianne developed, she grew more observant when she went to her friends' homes. She paid attention to the attitude of the parents to each other and their attitude towards their children. She noticed things, like the greetings that each gave to the other when one of them came in from work or had been away for a while.

Mark was a little alarmed when he witnessed the parents of his friends hugging them or kissing each other and thought that they were acting very strangely. When they started watching movies and television and saw amorous scenes between adults or children, they began to realise that some people behaved in this way. They never really stopped to wonder why their parents were different. Children accept certain things and questions only arise as they mature and grow up.

Their holidays were the best part of their growing years. They were usually spent up north with their maternal grandfather and family. Gramps, as they called him was a farmer who doted on his grandchildren. He had had a very happy life and although a widower for quite some years, his memories and his work kept him well adjusted and interested in all things. His unmarried daughter Anne, lived with him and kept the house, and helped with her twin sisters' four children, who lived nearby. She was thrifty and neat but generous with her family and never considered her life one of hardship or sacrifice. She was content. When Marianne and Mark were born, she welcomed them the same way as she had the other children. She was extremely patient, and the children sensed this and knew that in Anne they had a true friend.

Grace, Anne's twin, was married to John, an accountant and she worked part time in the local library. She was a motherly type of person and took life in her stride. Her four children were normal, very active, vocal and energetic. Their house was extremely noisy, always. As they got older, Marianne and Mark were entranced by their cousins.

Tom was the only son and farmed with his father. He was married quite late, to Millie, a lovely bubbly woman who charmed everybody. If Anne felt a bit put out when another woman entered the house, she quickly adapted and saw what a jewel her brother had married. In time they had two children, who were born after Mark. Tom was adored by his nieces and nephews, especially the young Mark. Summer holidays were totally complete with the tractor rides that Tom took Mark on.

Grace and John had a holiday cottage by the sea and part of many summer holidays were spent there. Marianne and Mark accompanied them as they got older. Life was so exciting then! Grace would ask them what they would like for dinner every evening, because they were on holidays, and the two little children could hardly believe that! Mark usually went for what the boys ordered but Marianne was quite unable to make a choice until gently guided by Grace. It was there that they both learned to swim, helped by their older cousins. The holidays seem to last for ages and being apart from their parents did not upset the two youngsters at all. At the end of the summer, either their mother or father drove up and collected them. They always needed new clothes as they seemed to grow a lot during these long summer days. When life at home got difficult, it was the thought of these holidays away that sustained them.

For the first couple of days back home, their father would ask general questions about how they got on. Mark would relate different activities excitedly, but Marianne noticed that her father did not really listen, it was as if he was just asking questions to keep the children talking. Marianne would look at her mother and notice her listlessness and lack of awareness that her children were now back home.

It took the children a couple of days to adapt after the noisy homestead they had left; the continual conversations, the banter and laughter. Their own house seemed so quiet and yet there was a certain tension there that they were aware of. Sometimes they heard raised voices from their bedrooms, but they quickly subsided, generally. Marianne used to wonder who was shouting at whom and why? Why was Gramps' house so easy to live in and so nice? Everyone got on with one another and there was always something to laugh at. Later when Tom's children were born, they were involved in sharing time with them and bringing them out in their buggy just as their older cousins had done for them.

Millie treated Marianne and Mark as if they were her own children and sometimes Marianne wished that Tom and Millie were her parents. She used to fantasize about it often. The two children saw only love and warmth between the two married adults in Gramps' house and it seemed perfectly normal and natural there. It was at the farm that the children learned about different relationships and love. Gramps' love for them was unconditional, even when Mark disobeyed or broke something; Anne's love was genuine and tender, even though she was a single lady; Grace was just Grace, lovable and they knew she regarded them as an extension to her own four.

Mark felt a yearning to go and live with this family as soon as he was grown up and had left school. He wondered if he could be a farmer also. Marianne loved the outdoor life and the walks in the moorland and mountains. Grace liked to paint in her free time and sometimes she would set off with the six children and some of their friends to spend the day up in the mountains. She would set up her easel and start painting and the children would play hide and seek or cowboys and Indians. Usually one of Grace's two girls and Marianne sat behind Grace and drew the landscape as Grace did. Marianne felt it must be wonderful to be an artist and decided that she would try and learn how to be one. There would always be a picnic basket, and everyone dived into Anne's baked goodies after a few hours. They never minded cold or showery days, it didn't stop the enjoyment or fun. The troop would return tired and red-cheeked after these excursions and ready for the big hot dinner that Anne would have prepared.

It was these halcyon days which made Marianne feel that her childhood was good and normal. The later dark days of sorrow and drama, which would come, could be wiped out with those wonderful early memories.

Chapter 2

Lizzie was so excited when she learnt that she was pregnant. She had not expected to get pregnant so soon after marriage. Lots of her friends were disappointed to find that this was not happening. Henry was thrilled also. They were very sensible people. Henry got a dietician to recommend a good well-balanced diet and was very solicitous of his new wife. His was a busy life but he made great efforts to be there for his wife and every evening would enquire about her day and insisted on washing the supper dishes, and he did all he could think of, to make her pregnancy comfortable.

Lizzie was a research assistant to a University professor. Mainly her job was checking information data, typing up papers and draft projects and arranging meetings with other professors. She often felt invisible, as she had nobody to really communicate with; no girly lunches or gossipy tea breaks. She was alone in an office with the daily comings and goings of her boss and the frequent changes of plans of projects and sometimes complete turnabouts in her document layouts. She was an adaptable woman and very patient and accommodating, so these many, frequent changes, did not really faze her.

She was happy in her new married life, loved the house that Henry already owned before he met her, and prided herself on her housekeeping abilities. She left the garden to Henry as she knew nothing about flowers or shrubs. Later, when his job got too busy, she suggested a gardener come once a fortnight, to help keep the garden in shape. She was surprised that he agreed so readily. She knew it would be money well spent as his job as a psychiatrist was very demanding and draining.

As her pregnancy progressed, she luxuriated in the attention and pampering her husband afforded her. She never felt ill at all and wondered about these women who complained of morning sickness and various other ailments. She regarded herself as a natural and enjoyed the different stages of pregnancy.

Coming to the end of her time, she appreciated the gentleness and consideration shown to her by Henry. He was so good, she thought, nothing was too much trouble. Even in the early stages, when she had such a yearning for pineapple, he had driven for miles looking for a store that stocked them! How they laughed about that at the time!

She went into labour the week that she was due, at three in the morning. Although they had both attended antenatal classes together, they were both a bit panicky. Of course, the labour went on for some time, as a first pregnancy usually does. In the end, she persuaded Henry to leave and go and have a cup of coffee and a sandwich. He had been there for hours by her side, holding her hand and mopping her brow and encouraging her. He had barely left when suddenly the contractions became much stronger. Then the midwife was telling her to push, push. She hadn't the strength to tell them to get her husband, or quite honestly, the will. She wanted this to be over. So it was, when Henry returned thirty minutes later, it was to find his wife holding their newborn daughter. He had cried then with relief and happiness and held the precious little bundle in his arms.

Yes, it was all so idyllic, Lizzie thought, looking back at that day. What had happened after that, she wondered? It had been a perfect pregnancy, perfect health, all scans and examinations, perfect. Then what? Why was there this feeling of emptiness and absolute nothingness? Why did she not feel anything for this little person they had brought into the world? All she felt was this huge anxiety. How would she cope? What did she know about babies? Henry assured her it was a traumatic time for first-time mothers and not to expect too much of herself. He encouraged her to try to breastfeed the baby, as did the nurses, but she could not even contemplate that.

When she went home, she spent hours just looking at the tiny baby. Her hands would shake when she was bottle feeding the child and she was terrified of bathing and changing her. She could only relax when

Henry came home. Then she would fall into a deep sleep. Upon waking, however, she would not feel rested. Only for Henry coping with the night feeds and bringing her a cup of tea in the morning, she would not have known where she was or that she was a mother.

Henry only realised something was amiss, when he got a hysterical call one afternoon in his office. Lizzie was incoherent and kept saying, 'I think she's dead.' She was sobbing so much he could not make much sense of what she was saying. Rushing home, sweating profusely, he found Lizzie on her knees beside the cot, sobbing. The baby was fast asleep and completely alright.

He helped his wife to bed and gave her a brandy to calm her. Soon, she was also asleep. Sitting in his study, he wondered what he should do. He made a telephone call to a good friend from medical school and they discussed the situation. He knew that it was probably postnatal depression, as a psychiatrist, he knew of various cases, but this was his wife! She had had a perfect pregnancy, why would this overcome her now? He could not believe that this would happen to him when he had done all that he could to help, during the pregnancy.

Lizzie recovered slowly. She was taking sedatives and knew exactly what was happening and understood that some women suffered the way that she did. It helped a little, but she was also ashamed.

Surely, she was stronger than this. She had wanted this baby, surely then, she should not have depression. She felt so guilty because of Henry. He was so good to her and now he must endure this. She felt that she had let him down badly.

Gradually she got back to normality. Now she was able to cook again and take care of the house, even if in a limited way. She soon found that having a drink during the day helped a lot. That way she could greet Henry when he came home and serve dinner and manage to give the baby her last feed. Henry insisted on getting up to tend her during the night.

Alcohol soon became her main helper. Why, there was nothing to worry about at all, once she had a couple of drinks. Once, Henry asked her on greeting her, if she had been drinking. She admitted it, but realised her breath gave the game away. Then she saw a billboard, saying that a certain brand of vodka left one breathless. At first, she did not get it, then suddenly it made sense. Vodka was then her main tipple and she made sure there was a supply in various places in the house. She felt guilty at times but reasoned that this was the only way she could function. As soon as she was well again, she would stop drinking.

When the baby was about three months, they had the christening. Most of her family travelled down. Afterwards, her sisters invited her to go and spend a bit of time with them and offered to help with

Marianne. Henry thought it was a great idea. They drove up in convoy with the family, complete with all the baby appliances. After a restful month, Lizzie felt much better and stopped drinking. In fact, she did not drink at all at the family home. Her two sisters took over the care of Marianne and Lizzie slept for hours at a time. She got her appetite back and put on a little weight. Baby Marianne grew and thrived. She was a bundle of joy, easy to manage, placid in the extreme and both sisters fought over her, and her cousins rushed home from school to push her out in her pram.

When Henry came up to visit, he was thrilled to see the change in Lizzie. He and her sisters had been in touch and they understood there had been a bit of depression and that was not so abnormal. After consulting with them now, they agreed that she seemed well, mentally and physically and that the baby was thriving.

Henry and his family returned home at the end of the week; Lizzie having been away almost six weeks. Life returned to normal and all were very happy.

Marianne was growing well and passed all her developmental tests. Lizzie was a proud mother. If she tried to remember the early months, it was all confused and fuzzy. She was still taking the prescribed medication as her doctor advised. After Marianne passed her first year of life, all was well in their little family. The trauma of the first few months gradually receded for Lizzie. Henry was the proud father, often seen pushing his baby daughter out in her buggy.

A year after the birth, Lizzie went back to Henry's medical friend Viv, who had treated her for her bout of postnatal depression, and they discussed her present situation and it was decided to discontinue the medication and see how she felt. Viv felt she should be reviewed every three months or so. Lizzie was happy with this outcome. Somehow being on medication meant that she was unfit as a mother and it bothered her. Henry and she had lots of discussions about this and finally she realised that this was a passing phase and it was now over. She was grateful for all the help she had got, although at the back of her mind she still felt that she should not have needed help. Her other friends all seemed normal and had not gone through this depression.

She went back to work when Marianne was eighteen months and started to work part time only, which suited her fine. Henry was not really in favour of her going back to work. His salary was enough, he felt. At the same time, he knew it would be beneficial mentally, for Lizzie to have a change of scenery. There was a very good creche not too far from their home. She liked the feeling of independence which she had taken for granted before Marianne's birth. Now, every day was an adventure, free to do whatever she liked. Mostly she liked to walk with the baby in the buggy and enjoy the fresh air and scenery, something she had never noticed before. She met regularly with her friends and made some new ones, through taking Marianne to the creche.

Life was gently settling into a rhythm. Henry was busy, working with patients, researching new medications and doing research with a fellow worker on Attention Deficit Disorder and its other half, Attention Deficit Hyperactivity Disorder. He had conferences to attend and at first, he worried about leaving Lizzie overnight. However, now and again her sister Grace would come and stay over while he was away, and by now, he felt, Lizzie was cured and whole again.

Weekends were a time of laziness and enjoyment. Some weekends were spent heading off in the car with a flask of tea, some sandwiches, baby food and no real plan of where they were going. Henry called these outings, 'Mystery Tours,' and Lizzie loved guessing where they might end up. They thought that their married life was idyllic in every way. After such outings there was nothing nicer than sitting at the fire in front of the television with a glass of wine, little Marianne fast asleep upstairs after all the fresh air.

CHAPTER 3

Life had been quite easy for Henry Dukes. His father was a successful businessman and his mother was an interior designer. He was the older of two children. His sister, Betts, was three years younger and a little 'slow' as they say. Not that she was handicapped in any obvious way, just quite literally a little slow. She was always smaller than her age group and he got used to acting as her guardian angel, as his mother used to call him. He was the brightest student in his class and was very competitive in all subjects. In sports he always excelled, but he was a good sport and took losing graciously. His father took great pride in his son's achievements.

He was taller than most in his class and knew he was good looking, from the attention he got from the girls in his group. He took it all in his stride and did not let it bother him. He was intent from an early age to go into medicine and his single mindedness blinded him to any romantic opportunities that were easily available. He got into medical school, of course, and went on to get a first-class degree. Deciding what to do then, caused him a spot of bother. He liked every aspect of medicine, but finally decided on psychiatry because of the admiration he felt for a professor he studied under. He did not realise how difficult it would be. However, he was a determined young man and battled on.

Home life was normal and good, his parents enjoyed social gatherings and Henry and Betts were always included. Betts began to show real talent in the kitchen and was a very adventurous cook. Her mother was delighted as she hated cooking and wondered, how on earth she had produced a daughter like Betts. She sent Betts to a renowned cookery school and the girl returned after four months quite an accomplished cook which delighted her parents, as they loved to entertain at home. Now they had a wonderful cook and Betts thrived in the atmosphere of success and praise heaped upon her. She also got a part time job cooking at the local school, three days a week. Her brother was proud and delighted with Bett's success, having once been a bit anxious about her prospects for a job. He felt real pride in his family, he felt that his was a perfect family.

Henry got on very well with his colleagues and was regarded as a good man to know. Willing to help and take responsibility for his work. His big problem arose in the second year of his psychiatric fellowship. On an overseas conference, funded by his college and accompanied by the professor he so looked up to, his peaceful life became disrupted when the professor appeared one night in his bedroom hotel. Not sure what to do, he waited and let her take the initiative.

He did not expect to be seduced. He felt totally at sea and helpless. She was very experienced sexually and he was still a virgin.

The following days of the conference were a confusing time for Henry. He was out of his depth completely and emotionally he was drained. What was he expected to feel, he wondered? The truth was, he was now totally disillusioned with this person that he had held in such high esteem. Suddenly his life felt belittled and dirty. She was his boss, who could he confide in? Each night she continued to dominate his bed and his mind began to feel fragmented. He longed to get home and regain control of his life. He had always been in control and this situation was abhorrent to him. He felt diminished, and demoralised.

Back at the hospital, her attention waned, thankfully. She was the model professor and was not going to risk her reputation by being found out in an illicit relationship. Henry once more became his normal self and was determined never to go to a conference which included her again. It was something that changed his attitude to women. He was never again attracted to women with strong personalities. He preferred the caring role that he had learned at home, looking after Betts.

So it was, that when he met Lizzie a few years later, he felt an immediate attraction. She was quiet and timid, never attention seeking. She blended easily into a crowd and never stood out. Even her clothing was modest and understated and her make up gentle and not obvious.

They got on well together even though they were quite different in their interests. Lizzie loved to read and listen to music. Her background was farming. She also loved all animals and went back home regularly to help her unmarried sister cope when it was harvest time and there were many extra people to feed. Henry was completely ignorant about life on a farm, but enjoyed talking to her father and brother, who he thought, were the salt of the earth. He felt welcome there, even if he knew that they thought he was a bit highbrow with all his medical knowledge. He was down to earth enough to go out with the father and son and Grace's husband to the local pub for an occasional drink.

Fatherhood agreed with Henry. He was confident handling baby Marianne and when depression struck Lizzie, he was well able to cope. He was rather shocked at the severity of her postnatal depression. It was totally unexpected, but he supposed, it usually is. Her family understood and helped all they could, but being almost four hours' drive away, it was difficult enough to manage. Work was demanding too, and he was beginning to feel desperate before Lizzie moved to her family home and family took over.

Now that things were back to normal, he was able to concentrate more thoroughly at work and did not have to worry about Lizzie like before. Weekends off duty meant they could go away and visit either the Dukes family or Lizzie's. The Dukes had a holiday home by the sea, and it was pleasant to get away now and again and enjoy being at the seaside with Marianne.

Henry often had meetings at the hospital, and his boss was usually present. At various times she had invited him to accompany her to conferences overseas. Henry used his sick wife as an excuse to avoid that, and from then on, he always had an excuse on hand. Professor Smythe knew that he was married of course, but it did not deter her from asking Henry. He was fearful that something would turn up that he would be obliged to attend. He felt frustrated about always feeling compromised and intimidated in her presence and was looking forward to the day he was no longer under her supervision. If he was a woman, he thought to himself, there would be hell to pay as sexual harassment would not be tolerated. He did not confide in any of his colleagues, thinking it would start something which he could not control, and no doubt there would be much merriment among his peers and perhaps even envy. They would want to start a 'Male Protest Movement', he thought, with a wry smile.

When Lizzie got pregnant with Mark, life changed again. Everything was fine and normal for six months after the birth, but then depression once again struck Lizzie and it was severe, like the first time. He spoke to Viv again, and a different medication was prescribed, which seemed to work well. However, having two children to care for now with Lizzie sick, was a headache. She refused to think of going home to her family now and wanted to stay where she was.

Henry found a helper, Ivy, to come every second day and mind the children or help in the house, depending on how Lizzie felt. Ivy was a motherly figure and easy going and had a grown family of her own. The children responded well to her and Henry usually experienced a calm household when he came home from work.

When Mark was about three years old, Lizzie became a little paranoid, as Henry thought. She was suspicious of his going to meetings or conferences or even just being late home from work. He did not know what was causing this, but supposed it was the medication. He made an appointment to see Viv and ask for her advice. She believed that it was all part of the postnatal depression but thought she should keep to the medication and see if that would help. He had been at university with Viv and was a little in awe of her knowledge and trusted her completely.

Henry was completing his training at this time and was struggling to cope with home life, especially on being interrogated every night on coming home. He knew there were jobs coming up that he would be eligible for and he dearly wanted to move to a different hospital. He was determined to move. There was a big psychiatric conference coming up in three months and he would have to attend and get recognition among other people in this line of work. He would be presenting a paper there on ADD and ADHD and it was an important step for him. Professor Smythe had been instrumental in getting sponsorship for this and her aegis in this, was all important to his future career. It was going to be a busy and very big meeting and he knew a lot of the other participants, so was not worried by Smythe's presence. There were too many people that she knew, attending.

It all went very well, and his paper was well received, and he got a lot of positive feedback about it. He was enjoying the feeling of being accepted and looked forward to his future. The meeting was attended by many different nationalities and mealtime was interesting. He spoke to many doctors who agreed with his approach to ADD and ADHD. He was invited to visit a few neighbouring countries to give talks, when he was available. He felt uplifted and very optimistic.

However, after dinner on the last night of the conference and very late in the evening, he discovered the professor waiting for him, in his room.

How she managed that, he did not know. She must have got a spare key from the reception desk. He was annoyed and embarrassed too. She laughed and held up a bottle of champagne.

'I want this evening to be a memorable one, Henry. My brightest and best student ever.' She went over to him and stood on tiptoe to kiss him. 'Now, Henry, please open this and let's enjoy ourselves.'

He opened the bottle and poured them both drinks. 'Professor Smythe, one only, you know that I am now a married man and father.' He said it lightly and with a smile but expected her to get the message.

'Please Henry, it's about time you dropped the professor and used my name, please call me Linda, I would love to hear your voice calling me that.' She toasted him and still smiling said, 'I have heard that you are looking at various positions around the county. You know, my endorsement can mean you will walk into any one of those positions you wish?' She smiled up at him, her head on one side.

He felt his heart constrict. This was the carrot. Oh, she was clever and crafty. He knew full well that if he did not get a reference from her, he was doomed. He took a sip of his drink. She moved towards him and said, 'Let's sit down and discuss the situation as I see it, will we?' As he sat down heavily, she got up and brought over the bottle of champagne and topped up their glasses.

Chapter 4

Lizzie was trying to get better and knew that eventually she would be well mentally. It was just so difficult. Every time she felt that things were improving, she got another setback. Then her life took a strange turn. It started late at night or sometimes, not so late; the telephone would ring and when she picked it up, she would hear someone breathing and then the phone would be put down. It always happened when Henry was late or at a meeting. At first, she put it down to someone dialing a wrong number, but then it happened too often. It was unsettling. When she mentioned it to Henry, he looked at her as if she had two heads.

'I can't tell you how many times that has happened to me, Lizzie, it's just a wrong number,' he smiled at her shaking his head. 'I guess I do it too, sometimes.'

Lizzie persisted, 'But do you not apologise when you do it?'

'Generally, I do, Lizzie, but if I hear a voice I don't want to hear, I sometimes just put the phone down.' He looked at her sympathetically, 'Just don't let it bother you, love.'

While he was away at the big psychiatric meeting, the calls were every night for the three nights he was away. The first night, she was asleep and then, waking out of a deep sleep, she groggily reached for the phone, thinking it was Henry, even though he rang every evening around six. He always said goodnight to Marianne who could now chat on the phone and loved doing so. Mark would just smile at the phone and ask, 'Dada coming home now?'

The second night it happened, she was awake and almost waiting for the call. When it came, she immediately asked, 'Who is this, why are you calling me?' The only reply was a muffled laugh and then the phone went dead. Of course, sleep was impossible after these calls. The third night, the call came at three in the morning. She looked at the phone and wondered if she should just ignore it. After ten rings, it stopped, and she relaxed. She was just dropping off to sleep when it rang again. This time she lifted the receiver and stayed silent. The sounds at the other end were of glasses clinking and a woman laughing. Then the call ended. She went down to the kitchen and made herself a hot drink. At this rate she would get no sleep and the only way she could cope with everything, was by getting a good nine or ten hours of sleep.

When Henry came back the following day, it was to find Lizzie in a state of confusion. He asked her if she had taken her medication and she snapped that she had, 'Fat lot of good it's doing me!'

When the children were in bed, he sat down beside her and asked her gently what was wrong and what did she think her main problem was? Turning towards him, he was startled to see how angry she looked.

'It's all these phone calls that I keep getting, Henry. I don't know how long more I can put up with it.' She began to cry, and he put his arms around her, rocking her gently. He told her he would try to find out who was making the calls.

'I have a good idea, Lizzie. When I am not here, leave the phone off the hook. Wouldn't that be the answer?'

Lizzie blew her nose and said, 'And suppose you need to get in touch with me, or I need to get in touch with you?'

'Then I'll just use the mobile, not many people have your number, do they?'

Lizzie thought about all the people that had her number, schools, clinics, all the forms you must provide your mobile number on. She said nothing but nodded silently.

'We can try it, I suppose,' she mumbled. 'I feel like telling the police about it, to be honest.'

This alarmed Henry. He reasoned with her that they could hardly do anything about these calls unless they had a number to check, or if a threat was received. Lizzie was left feeling unassured and fearful. He was inclined to disbelieve her of course. This postnatal depression caused a lot of problems, real and imaginary.

The rest of the week passed uneventfully. There were no more silent phone calls. In the hospital, Henry got a lot of compliments for his paper and he began to look more at the jobs on offer. He was quite fearful too and did not confide much in his colleagues. He sent his CV to a good many nearby hospitals and prepared to wait patiently for a call to be interviewed.

At her next appointment with Viv, she related her worries about the silent phone calls and wondered if she was going mad. Viv laughed at her and said of course she was not mad, but someone might just be having a lark.

'Best to pay no attention, Lizzie, just don't answer the phone when Henry is not there. Whoever it is will soon tire and turn his attention to someone else.' She reviewed Lizzie's file and decided that she would need to be kept on medication until this slight paranoia was under control.

Ivy was a godsend to Lizzie and was the most obliging person that she had ever met. Mark was mad about her and ran into her arms every morning when she appeared, always smiling, at the door. He was now in his last year of playschool. Marianne was in proper school of course, and quite a bossy little lady around her small brother.

Summer was here and it was time for holidays. Lizzie decided it was time to visit her father and family up north. The phone calls had ceased now for a few months. She was feeling fit and well and told Henry she would drive up in her car and when the weekend came, he could come up when he was free. She intended to stay a couple of weeks in the country and enjoy the fresh air and Anne's cooking. It would also be lovely for Marianne and Mark to get to know their older cousins.

Life was as usual on the farm, always busy and bustling. Her dad was pleased to see his youngest daughter and his small grandchildren. The weather was beautiful, and Lizzie felt for the first time in ages, elated and glad to be alive.

On her second night, her mobile rang at midnight and she was puzzled, as Henry had rung much earlier in the evening. She whispered 'Hello, love,' as she did not want to wake the two sleeping children who were sharing the room with her. There was only the familiar deep breathing and then the call ended. Angrily she turned off her phone and lay down and tried to go to sleep. How could this be starting again, she asked herself. She lay still, trying to relax and stop herself from thinking about it. She decided she would switch off her phone each evening after Henry called.

When Henry call her on her mobile the next evening, she told him about it. He was silent for so long, she asked if he was still there. He said he was and would see her in three days' time. He also told her to switch off the phone during the night. Again, he mentioned her medication and asked if she was taking it as prescribed.

'Of course, I am, I'm not geriatric, you know!' was the reply she bitterly spat down the line. He regretted at once having mentioned it. He had mentioned the paranoia and phone calls to Viv, and she said that sometimes, the medication could have temporary side effects and not to worry, she was keeping an eye on things.

At the end of the week, Henry made the journey up north and was relieved to see Lizzie and the children again. The children loved the outdoor life and followed Gramps around all day. He was so patient with them, showing them the chickens and collecting the eggs and explaining how the chickens laid the eggs that they liked for their breakfast. They looked with amazement and a bit of fear too, at the sow that Gramps had in a special pen. They adored helping to hold the bucket with the milk for the calves and hearing them guzzle it all down. Mark could be heard from up at the house, laughing down in the yard in delight.

It was up at the house that Lizzie was struck with a vague suspicion. It was so bizarre that she reproached herself crossly. The niggling thoughts persisted however and affected her mood.

In the evening, she was quite abrupt with Henry and did not engage with him in the talk around the dinner table. When Henry asked her if she would like to go out for a drink at the local pub, she declined, even though Grace and John were going. He felt a bit hurt, as there was no excuse. There were Gramps and Anne to mind the children. Tom and Millie were away with their two little children.

She lay awake thinking about how the calls only came when Henry was away. Was it a coincidence she wondered or was it possible that Henry had something to do with them? She was annoyed with herself for even thinking like this. If this was someone else, I would accuse them of paranoia, she reasoned. Still, it was strange.

When Henry came to bed later, she pretended to be asleep and did not move when he put his arm around her. She heard him sighing as he turned on his side away from her.

The following week, when she returned home with the children, the first thing she did was to buy a bottle of vodka. If it helped me before, then it will surely help me again, she thought. At least it might relax her a bit instead of being on tenterhooks the whole time. That night she had the best night's sleep in a long time but felt a bit groggy when she awoke. I must be careful, she thought, not to overdo the vodka. But she felt more cheerful than she had in ages.

So, life continued. Her suspicions came and went for a time. She tried to do without medication but that was unsuccessful. When she stopped the medication, she needed more alcohol; when she resumed medication the paranoia and suspicion became worse. It seemed that she was sinking into a great big black hole and the chances of climbing out of it were diminishing daily. Eventually, she persuaded Viv to try a different stronger antidepressant and see if that would help. The phone calls, always silent, still came irregularly. She knew that both her doctor and her husband did not understand and did not believe her.

Now and again Henry would bring the children up north to her father and Anne, to give her a break and a chance to sleep. She could never get enough sleep. It became a pattern over time, the children being brought up and left with their granddad and aunties and cousins by themselves. But they always loved going up there and returned full of life and energy.

Lizzie relished the peace and quiet of the empty house when they were away. She could get out of bed when she wished. She could also imbibe her alcohol in freedom. Ivy did not interfere with her but did her work and left early as arranged.

Chapter 5

Henry felt more alienated than ever from his wife. They had not been physically intimate for so long and he did not know how to approach the matter. He suggested a break, a weekend away, just the two of them and asked Ivy if she would babysit. He thought it would be received well and was puzzled when Lizzie became agitated.

'What sort of a mother would I be to leave the children for a weekend?' she demanded. 'Ivy has her own family you know, and what would she think of me wanting to leave them?'

Henry thought Ivy would understand that they needed time together and it was not as if the children did not like Ivy, they only loved her, he remonstrated.

In the end, he got her to agree to a break away, to a spa hotel where they could luxuriate in saunas and massage and simply eating what they wanted, when they wanted. Lizzie was worried about how she would hide her bottle of vodka from Henry.

Ivy agreed and was looking forward to having the two to herself and assured Lizzie that she would ring twice a day and if there was anything at all worrying her, she would ring them, day or night. The two children hugged their parents at their leaving and waved goodbye without a sign of a tear, if fact they acted as if it was a great adventure to be left with Ivy.

The hotel was two hours' drive away and was big and impersonal looking, the way most hotels are, these days. Corridors with doors numbered, carpeted and silent. Henry was sorry he had not researched hotels more carefully. He thought a family run hotel would have been better, now that he saw this one. They discussed this, and Lizzie agreed that big hotels were more sanitized and had less atmosphere.

'However, we're here now, so we had better make the most of it, I suppose,' she said smiling.

Henry was relieved that she was so upbeat about it. He was the moaner, it seemed. They booked their treatments and agreed to have a walk first in the gardens. There were many people there, some for the golf and some just relaxing in the spa. It was all lovely and relaxing. Lizzie enjoyed the feeling of being pampered and wondered why she had not thought of doing something like this before now.

Dinner was beautifully served and neither of them could fault it. Lizzie had a vodka before dinner, having been asked by Henry what she would like. For once, he did not mention her medication. They had a glass of wine with their dinner and retired to the lounge for coffee.

When Lizzie came back from the bathroom, she found Henry engaged in conversation with a beautiful woman, elegantly dressed. As Lizzie approached, Henry turned to her and said 'Lizzie, this is Professor Smythe, my old tutor.'

Lizzie proffered her hand and said 'Hello, Professor Smythe.'

'Oh really, please call me Linda,' she smiled, 'I've told your husband to, many times, but he is such a shy gentleman. I have just been congratulating him on his new appointment, he is very much missed in my department, I can't tell you how much.' All the time she was speaking, she was gazing up at Henry adoringly and had her hand on his arm. Lizzie began to feel uncomfortable and was not sure if she was expected to say something. Henry quickly moved towards Lizzie and put his arm around her shoulders and said, 'Well Professor, nice meeting you here, but we have had a busy day and are tired.' He moved away and walked towards the exit leading Lizzie by the hand.

Upstairs, Lizzie said, 'Henry, you were rather abrupt with that lady, weren't you, or was it just my imagination?'

Henry turned and looked at her and said, 'Lizzie, you don't know the half of it, and she is not a lady.'

As Lizzie started to ask more, Henry put up his hand and said, 'Please Lizzie, never mention her name to me again.'

Henry was upset at having met Linda and tonight of all nights. Why had she been in the same place? It was not fair, and he had wanted so much for this weekend to be special. He felt his mood change and anger set in. How dare the woman approach him and simper at him in front of Lizzie, as though they were friends.

The next morning after breakfast, the two went for a brisk walk in the wooded area beside the hotel. Lizzie had slept well and was unaware that Henry was awake most of the night fretting about his former boss. Henry was anxious in case the Smythe woman was still about and kept his eyes watchful. He met a couple of old friends on the way back and was invited to join them in a round of golf. He declined and explained he was not here for the golf and anyway had not brought his golf clubs. His friends said there was no problem, they could share. Lizzie turned to Henry and told him to have a round or two if he wished, his golfing shoes were in the boot of their car and that she would be fine and would go for a massage. He really did not want to go but felt obliged especially as Lizzie had urged him to.

Lizzie enjoyed her massage thoroughly and afterward went into the sunroom to relax and doze. After some time, she felt someone sit down beside her on the next lounger and felt her arm being patted. Opening her eyes, she saw Linda stretched out in her robe beside her.

'Don't let me disturb you Liz,' she said. 'We all need a little pampering now and again, don't you think?' She sighed and closed her eyes. 'How are you keeping these days Liz, all the problems cleared up?'

Lizzie was taken aback. What did this stranger know of her problems?

'I am fine, thank you.' she replied stiffly and wondered what to do next. Should she just get up and leave?

'I am so glad to hear it. You know, poor Henry was quite worried about you. He and I were very close in the past, you probably know? I am sure he told you all about me, did he?'

'Actually, no he didn't,' Lizzie heard herself reply as though from a distance.

'Naughty boy, I suppose being a bit old fashioned, he is not as open as I would expect most young people of his generation to be, about things like that. Ah! What a beautiful man in bed, as you must know yourself.' Linda stretched herself out, rather like a cat and looked at Lizzie, slant eyed. 'I must arrange more conferences away, I know you don't mind sharing him,' she laughed.

Lizzie got up quickly and without saying a word, left the solarium and returned to her room. She could hardly believe what she had just heard. She sat on the bed in a daze, still in her robe, shaking with shock and anger. Eventually she got up and took out her bottle of vodka and poured herself a stiff drink.

Henry returned to the hotel after an hour. He had not wanted to stay any longer and did not want to meet with his friends later for drinks. He thought he would like a swim in the pool and then have lunch with Lizzie. He was shocked when he went to their room. Lizzie was sitting in an armchair with an empty bottle of vodka on the floor, crying. He ran across the room and knelt beside her, 'What's wrong, Lizzie?' He had to keep asking as she just shook her head, over and over and eventually she just stared at him and said 'Linda.'

It took two hours to calm her down, and as she was inebriated, he had to repeat everything a few times to get through to her.

Eventually he understood the exchange that Linda and Lizzie had and was horrified and disgusted. He tried to tell her he never had an affair with her and that seemed to make her more hysterical. So, he tried to explain what his situation with Linda had been, and how it was before he met her. Lizzie would have none of it. She knew it was not only years ago. How could she ever trust him again? She suddenly stopped short, appeared quite sober now and said. 'Of course, now I understand about those phone calls. It was her, wasn't it? It must have been her, they only started after you were away at that recent conference, when you presented your paper.'

Henry felt his stomach lurch. Why did he not connect those calls? Was it perhaps because he did not really believe Lizzie and thought that she was paranoid? He silently thought about their last exchange in his bedroom, when Linda saw her way to coax him to give in. She had thought that the promise of a good position would sway him. He saw her again in his mind, when he told her what he thought of her and told her to get out of his room.

'You are a sick, sad woman,' he had shouted at her, 'and a disgrace to your profession.'

As Linda had looked at him in amazement, he decided to throw in a bit more insult to convince her.

'What makes you think that you are even attractive, or desirable to any intelligent male? You are a desperate silly and shallow bitch, and you probably will always be one.'

He was heading for the bedroom door at this stage and held the door open. There was no movement from the sofa where Linda still sat open mouthed. So, he returned, and roughly took her by the arm and forcefully marched her across the room and literally pushed her out of the doorway. He was vaguely aware of someone passing but was too preoccupied to take much notice. He did not give a damn who saw it happen. He felt so angry.

As she stood outside the door, swaying slightly, she said quietly, 'Henry, you have just signed your death warrant regarding your career.'

He had slammed the door and stood with his back to it, breathing heavily. Drained, he made his way to the sofa and sat down, his brain was now numb. That's it then, he thought, she will never give me a reference for any job that requires one. What is going to happen to me?

She never did give him a reference, he learned the truth of that, when he applied for various positions. He was fortunate to be accepted in his present one, on his own merit and because of the paper he had presented at that conference. When he met other medical people in the service or even in administration, their eyes sort of slid beyond him when they met professionally, as though he was an embarrassment. He now understood why. Heaven only knows what stories and slanders, Smythe had spread about him. As he remembered it all, the bitterness returned, and he looked down sadly at his wife and knew that she too had suffered at the hands of this woman.

Lizzie was crying again, and Henry tried to take her in his arms, but she pushed him away. He was exasperated and angry.

'Lizzie, I tell you, that woman is poison, and nobody could possibly love or even like her, I could really kill the bitch, for hurting you.'

Shortly after this, Lizzie fell asleep and slept for four hours. Then it was time to pack up and return home. As for being a blissful quiet time for the two of them, it proved to be a total and utter disaster.

During the silent two-hour drive home, Henry wondered whether his marriage would be able to survive Linda's interference. How could he make Lizzie believe that he hated the woman and only had that one bad experience with her, years before he had met her?

He had heard about and often recommended counselling for patients who experienced tough times in their marriage. He wondered whether it would help them. He knew that he would feel humiliated if he chose that path, especially if he met people who were involved, that he knew. Anyway, Lizzie probably would not agree to such a thing. She was very private and even, restrained, in her friendship with the girls she knew.

CHAPTER 6

The following months were busy for Henry at work. The number of referrals increased, and his reputation spread rapidly. Not many other psychiatrists had as many teenage patients, not too many people were comfortable treating teenagers. He was settling into the job well and had the admiration and support of the staff at the hospital.

He was being pressured to start a private clinic for those parents who were disinclined to attend the hospital for one reason or another. An office in the town was available and he was tempted. Unable to have a conversation with Lizzie about his work, he asked a colleague what he thought about it. Given the reassurance that he needed, he started to make plans to open a private clinic the following September. It would not interfere with his hospital hours and would probably involve working a couple of evenings a week.

Lizzie was busy now with school runs and was part of the Parent/Teacher committee. She felt that finally, she was contributing something important. Her medication continued but she felt she was coping well. Her drinking continued too however, and now she knew that she would not be able to cope without her bottle of vodka. At first, it lasted a full week, but after six months she was using three to four bottles a week. She was clever though, she thought, not one person really suspected as she was very careful. She would not get behind the wheel of her car if she had taken a drink. But as soon as her duty ended, and the children were at home and her going out for the day was done, it was Vodka Time. By the time Henry came home, she and the children were usually in bed.

She had changed her bedroom one weekend when Henry was on duty. She now slept in the guest room, which had an ensuite. No explanation was given, and Henry said nothing. He felt hurt and shaken, however.

She started leaving notes for Henry if something needed repairing or seen to. The children were used as messengers when they were all at home. 'Tell your Dad that dinner is ready, Marianne,' or 'Mark, will you remind your Dad that there is football tomorrow night and Mummy is busy?'

As Marianne grew older, she was a bit rebellious, especially if she was on her iPod. She wondered why on earth her mother could not relay her own messages. Honestly! How lazy parents are, she would mutter under her breath. Her father also started the same system of communication. 'Tell Mummy that I'll be working late at the clinic tomorrow, will you Marianne?'

Mealtime became a silent affair for the two adults. The children would chatter away and tell their parents about their day and ask questions. They really did not seem to notice that the adults did not communicate with each other. Soon it became the norm.

This year, half term holiday was going to be spent up at the farm. The children were looking forward to it but at the same time, would have preferred to stay at home and go trick/ treating with their friends. The farm was great in summer but very quiet during the autumn. However, maybe their cousins would have something exciting for them to do.

'Why don't you come and stay too, Mum', asked Mark. 'We could have some fun, and maybe go into town with Gramps and go to the sheep fair or something'. Poor Mark never remembered which time of year the animal fairs were held, but thought it would be nice if she was there.

'I might just travel up with you and return again with daddy. I really need the time to sort out the Christmas fair, which will need to be organised before term starts again. You know, the Christmas party stuff and awards and general Christmas programme, which every child enjoys. The Santa grotto, that you love, and candlelit carol programme. These things are all arranged beforehand, at half term, and the parent's committee does all that.' She smiled at the children. 'We mums, and dads do really work at it, you know?'

Mark and Marianne nodded enthusiastically. Christmas was their favourite time of year and parents in their school really went all out for the celebrations. They would all drive up to the farm and later at the end of the week, they would collect them, and that was fine by both children. Gramps was a doting granddad and very humerous for his age and willing to put himself out for his grandchildren.

The Saturday came for their journey and Lizzie woke with a hangover. She felt sick and told Henry she would not be able to travel with them. Their bags had been packed the day before and they went off highly excited with Henry. He was annoyed and disappointed that Lizzie would not go with them. He still respected his wife and would not risk a confrontation with her. It would achieve nothing. He also did not want the children to be witnesses to any unpleasantness. He knew firsthand of the problems that children suffered from witnessing warring parents. Really, he thought to himself, more than once; if one needs a licence to own a dog, should not the same apply for the much more important job of having children?

Lizzie went to the hairdressers that afternoon and decided that she must cut down on the drinking. She met three of her pals for coffee at four o'clock and they discussed what they would be doing for half term. When she left them, she felt very alone and empty. They were all so connected to their husbands and families and she was so different to them. It hurt her and made her feel inferior in some way. Why am I different, she wondered? Was it because her husband had been having an affair with his boss? Was it all in the past? No, not for a moment had she believed that. The Smythe woman had a hold over her husband, and she felt inadequate and belittled by it. The medication and alcohol certainly helped, and she was able to cope with her life. It was just Henry she could not cope with.

She did not feel like cooking and decided to go to the local cafe and have a fish and chip supper. In the adjoining supermarket, while buying a bottle of vodka, she bumped into Viv. She explained that Henry was dropping the children to the farm and suggested that they both go and have supper out. Viv agreed and said that she had not had fish and chips out for ages. She bought a bottle of white wine for them to have, and giggling like schoolgirls, they made their way to the cafe.

The two of them got on so well and enjoyed their meal together. Viv was always a great person for a laugh and the jokes came fast and furious. Lizzie had not laughed as much in ages. As they looked over the dessert menu and decided on the pavlova, they both looked up at the same time as two more customers entered and sat across the room from them. They both stopped talking and stared. It was Linda Smythe with a youngish man. She obviously did not see them, and they were sitting side by side in an alcove, very lovey, dovey. Lizzie stared, and her face dropped. Viv noticing, asked, 'What are you thinking, Lizzie?'

Lizzie kept silent. Viv pursued the matter, 'Mutton dressed as lamb, don't you think, Lizzie, and he is the lamb, being led to the slaughter.' Viv started to giggle and then it became a snorting laugh and then the two of them started to laugh and could not stop.

The two love birds did not hear, luckily, and continued to gaze into each other's eyes, adoringly. Viv wiped her eyes with a tissue and blew her nose. 'You know Lizzie that she is a nymphomaniac and a man-eater?' She kicked Lizzie under the table. 'She can't help it, and the students she catches in her net, are unable to escape as she is their boss!' She started to giggle again but stopped when she saw the look of pain on Lizzie's face. 'What's wrong, Lizzie?'

Lizzie looked down and picked at her paper napkin. She looked up at Viv with brimming eyes.

'I know about her, Viv. She snared my Henry.'

Viv gaped at her and said, 'I can't believe it, Lizzie. Poor Henry.'

'It's true, Viv, he told me about it, that it happened while he was her student. But she told me herself, that she met him at the big conference a couple of years ago, and I think the affair never really ended.'

Viv stared at Lizzie with her mouth open. 'Well… I don't know what to say, Lizzie, except that it certainly would not have been Henry's idea. She would not be the ideal woman for any man that I know. A veritable horse-face!'

Her face dissolved into merriment and despite her loathing, Lizzie could not control the giggles and laughter that erupted. The two of them collapsed into a fit of uncontrollable laughter. People at other tables looked over at them and smiled at their seeming joy. Eventually, Linda also looked over and if looks could kill, they would have been dead.

They had their dessert and coffee, but for Lizzie, the evening was spoiled. Viv kept the humour and jokes coming but she could see that Lizzie was shaken. Leaning over, she placed her hand over Lizzie's and said, 'Lizzie, whatever you imagine was between Henry and that she-wolf, is absolutely nothing, I can promise you that. You know your husband! Can you imagine that he would ever want anything to do with that piece of work?'

Lizzie nodded glumly. 'I keep telling myself that, but still she has the power to upset me, you know?'

She told Viv about the meeting in the hotel solarium and the disgusting way that Linda had spoken about Henry. Viv was shocked and quietened down.

'Liz, just remember that you are worth a thousand times more than *that* woman, and Henry is a gentleman, a wonderful man of moral integrity. You have nothing to worry about.'

Viv insisted on paying the bill and gave Linda a cheery, 'Good evening, Professor,' on her way past the table. Lizzie did not acknowledge the woman at all. Viv was delighted to see the young student, whom she recognised, redden with embarrassment.

When they got outside, she linked arms with Lizzie and escorted her to her car. They got a fit of giggles again when Viv told Lizzie who the student was and how she knew his mother and how mortified he must be.

'You have to pity her Lizzie, baby snatching and she well into menopause.'

They laughed again and promised they would repeat the evening soon again as it was so entertaining.

As soon as she reached home, Lizzie opened the bottle of vodka and began drinking in earnest. There was a message on her phone to say that Henry and the children had arrived safely, and all were well at the farm. It was too late to reply and anyway, what could she add to that?

It was in the early hours when she staggered up the stairs to bed and got undressed. As she got into bed her mobile phone rang. Oh, for heaven's sake, she thought, I got your message. She wearily answered 'Yes,' and then the familiar breathing started again. It had been so long that she had almost forgotten. She listened intently and heard the whispered, 'He's mine, you know.' Lizzie shut off the call and turned off her mobile. The bitch, she thought, is still at it. What is wrong with that woman?

When she eventually fell asleep, she kept waking up in a distressed state. That was the night the dreams started, and they were extremely disturbing. They always involved a shadowy figure that lurked behind her and even when she ran, she could not escape. There was nowhere safe for her. The figure was all powerful and she woke from them, drenched in sweat and wild-eyed.

Chapter 7

Lizzie decided she could not stay in the house with Henry when he returned after dropping the children to the farm. She made some phone calls to her three friends who she was working with for the Christmas presentation and explained that she had to leave suddenly. She quickly packed a case and told Henry she would return at the end of half term. He did not have time to even discuss anything with her. She just took off. He sighed as he watched her car shoot out of the driveway and wondered again if the medication was having any effect on her mood swings. He went up to his study wearily and turned on his computer. He spent the rest of the afternoon, looking up new medication for continual postnatal depression. He was himself depressed at his findings. The phone rang, and he picked it up sighing, supposing that Lizzie had forgotten something. It was a friend of hers, Kate, who lived on the next street to them. She told him that she knew Lizzie had left for the country but wondered if Lizzie had left anything for her, as she had expected a parcel of books to be delivered to her house before she left. Henry told her that Lizzie had left nothing and had not mentioned the books but had left rather hurriedly.

'Kate, if you like, I'll have a look around for the parcel and drop it to you.'

Kate said that she would collect them and not to worry about it, she felt the books might be in the garage as it would be quite a big parcel. Henry told Kate he would search and let her know if he found them.

There was a pause at the other end of the phone, then Kate asked, 'Henry, I hope you don't mind me asking, but is Lizzie, you know, is she alright?'

Henry looked at the phone and then replied, 'Kate, what exactly do you mean?'

'Oh my God, Henry, I didn't mean it to sound so inquisitive. It's just that a few of us are sort of worried about her. Sometimes she seems to be on another planet. Now, don't get me wrong, we all love Lizzie. We don't gossip or speak badly of her, it's just that we are genuinely concerned about her.'

Henry felt his stomach churning. Trying to sound calm and soothing, he explained gently that of course she was improving after the postnatal depression and he was certain that shortly she would be back to her old self. He knew these women and their husbands, decent people all of them.

There was another pause at Kate's end and Henry asked whether she was still there. Kate coughed and said, 'Henry, I hope you will take this the right way, but….are you aware that she is drinking quite significantly?'

Henry felt his chest constrict. He had no idea that Lizzie was drinking while on her medication. He sighed and admitted to Kate that he had not realised that. Kate was apologetic and Henry said, 'No Kate, really, you are sensible and caring to tell me. I will have to talk with her and her doctor. She should not be drinking while on medication, she should not have a drink at all, even socially. Thank you so much for being a good friend to her. Don't ever hesitate to contact me again, we both have Lizzie's wellbeing as a priority.'

Kate said goodbye sadly, and said she hoped all would be well. Henry put his head in his hands after the call and wondered what on earth he could do. Kate obviously did not know about the state of his marriage with Lizzie. He later rang Viv and said that he would really appreciate a meeting as soon as possible. She set up an appointment for lunch time Monday. He then went to look in the garage where he found the box of books which Kate needed. He delivered them straight away to Kate's house and declined an offer of a cup of coffee.

Later that Sunday evening, he contacted some colleagues from work and asked two trusted friends out for a drink. These were outsiders and would not be acquainted with his old colleagues in Linda's department. They were single and very interested in their work. There was never time for a social chat in work hours. The day was just not long enough. The three were all talkative and Henry was relieved to be out of the house and in a normal environment for once. The lads chatted and discussed local sporting events and happenings. Medicine was left at home, which was a relief for them.

At eleven o'clock they got up to leave and the younger of the three said that he was going to the jazz club further up the street. Henry asked him if it was good there, as he liked jazz. After a short discussion on jazz, the three of them ended up going to the club. The place was jam packed and it was rather dark inside. The music sounded terrific. The three found a table eventually and Henry ordered drinks. The place was buzzing and suddenly there were people that they knew from work and elsewhere stopping to chat to the men. The atmosphere was electric, and Henry mused at how this can so change your mood, and after feeling tired and old all day, he suddenly felt alive and invigorated. The drinks flowed the music played and the world became a bit fuzzy for Henry. He knew he should now go home, but to what? For the first time in ages, he was enjoying himself. At one stage he was having a very deep conversation with someone about the difference between jazz and blues. There was now quite a big crowd around the table and a few girls were sitting beside his two friends. Henry was standing in the crowd, all chatting away loudly, because of the music. Leaving to go to the toilet he fumbled his way a bit, ordering more drinks as he passed the bar. On his return his friends had now moved up towards the toilets and he stayed with them. There were still people coming into the club. Their original place was taken over by a huge throng of people, mostly women. He listened to the music and joined in the conversation with his friends and others that had joined them. When he finished his drink, he said that he must go. They nodded and asked if he was alright to drive. Shaking his head, he told them he would get a taxi.

He felt light and happy and like a boy again. He fell into bed and slept like a baby. It was only in the morning, and could not find his phone, that he realised that he had left his phone at the jazz club and cursed himself for being stupid. He rang his friends in the hope that they had taken it for him, but they had not. Well, it had probably slipped out of his pocket at the jazz club and he would only be able to check, when it opened Monday night. That was a nuisance to be sure. He showered and got a taxi to the club where he picked up his car and went on to work.

At lunch time, he remembered his appointment with Viv and rang her. They arranged to meet for lunch so that they could return to work quickly and not miss any other patients. He told Viv about Kate's phone call and asked how it might affect her medication. Viv said that alcohol was expressly advised against as it could cause serious consequences in conjunction with the type of antidepressant which Lizzie was on. She looked at Henry and told him that he would need to explain that to her. When Henry shook his head, Viv looked at him in surprise.

'What you need to know, Viv, is that Lizzie and I are not getting on at all and are hardly communicating with each other. It has been like this for quite a while and it pains me to have to admit this to you, an old friend. I just don't know what to do anymore.'

Viv sighed and shook her head. 'Henry, I am so sorry to hear this, I am so fond of you both and your children are so special, you know? But as a friend to both of you, I cannot stand by and say nothing. I will ring Lizzie and get her to come in, or, maybe just call by on a friendly visit. What do you think?'

Henry agreed that whatever she did, something must be done and soon. He thought of Lizzie up at the farm and knew he could not let her drive back with the children, in case she had been drinking. Another problem, he sighed! He would have to ring Grace and get her opinion of everything. He could no longer keep it a secret from the family.

They both returned to work and Henry tried to clear his mind and concentrate on the patients who were scheduled to meet him. There was a meeting tonight with the Mental Health Services people and he had to attend that. Luckily it was not a night when he had a private clinic. Then he remembered that he must not forget to call to the jazz club and ask about his phone. He went home for a sandwich and had a quick shower before going out again. On his way to the meeting he passed the club and was relieved to see it was open. He went in and explained about his phone. The place was quiet with just a few drinkers. The music did not start until around nine. He went over to where he remembered they sat and looked around. The barman came over to help him and put a few more lights on. There it was, down behind one of the leather-backed seats, just as he had suspected. Relieved, he checked it and returned to his car and drove on to the meeting.

    The hall was crowded with staff from a few surrounding hospitals and clinics and day care centres. Henry greeted those people that he knew and out of the corner of his eye he saw Linda and was determined not to look in her direction. The meeting began and very soon it was apparent what it was all about. The Department of Health was as usual, strapped for cash and had decided that by amalgamating certain areas, they could save money and, they thought, provide a more efficient service. Henry saw a lot of people shaking their heads and looking at each other. Linda, the professor, was seated at the top table with the other important decision makers and was looking very positive and happy. Henry deliberately would not look at her and knew she was trying to catch his eye.

The meeting went on and on and the audience was getting tired of the pomposity of some of the speakers at the top table and their opinionated ideas of how the mental health service should be run. At the break for tea, Henry turned around and came face to face with Linda, who beamed up at him.

'Henry, the very man I want to see! What do you think of the new ideas floating around? I really want your department and mine to link up. I think we would have the best department of the lot. We are both in adolescent and child psychiatry and it would be the best of both worlds, don't you think?'

'No Linda, I do not think it a good idea at all.' Henry looked her straight in the eye and said, 'Bigger departments do not necessarily mean more efficiency, as I am sure you know.' He took a deep breath at his boldness of speech.

She smiled at him as though he had not spoken and asked him to imagine the input they would have into their research. She knew Henry was very interested in any research that pertained to his speciality. He was always researching when not treating patients or tutoring students.

Henry felt himself redden in anger and outrage, remembering how her name had always appeared on his papers, although she had not contributed anything to them. That happened because he was a student in her department, and it was her right. He put down his cup and saucer and tried to control the tremor in his hand. Glaring at her he said, 'Linda, those days are over, pounce on some other poor fool of a student.'

He turned on his heel and left the room and building and went home thoroughly annoyed. Why did he let her annoy him so much? Ignoring her would be much more hurtful to that woman. He should have agreed with her and strung her along for months.

He sat in his study and suddenly realised that he had not rung Lizzie since she left for the farm. He reached for his phone and dialled her number, checking his watch to make sure it was not too late to ring her.

Chapter 8

Lizzie enjoyed being alone in the car on the long drive up to the farm. It gave her freedom to think about things as she bowled along on near empty roads. She really must spend all her free time with her children and do different activities with them. She knew that they had asked about a visit to the zoo and she had really ignored them. She was going to stop drinking, for sure, and had not brought a bottle of vodka with her. She felt determined and motivated and really looked forward to getting her life back on track. She was not going to let the phone calls anger her again. Being in the same house as Henry was difficult. Every time she saw him, she was reminded of his unfaithfulness to her. It was like a continuous needle sticking into her, no matter how much she drank.

She stopped halfway for a coffee and rang Anne to explain that she was on her way.
'That's wonderful Lizzie, we are all going on a trek tomorrow and I know that the kids will be thrilled to have you there.'

Anne was surprised, as Henry had said nothing about her coming up when he left. 'I will not tell the two that you are coming, we'll keep it as a surprise.'

There was great joy and excitement when she drove into the farmyard. Mark jumped up and down with glee and Marianne smiled shyly at her mother.

They all sat around the fire after supper and chatted animatedly until bedtime. Gramps was happy to see his Lizzie and thought that she had put on a little weight and looked well. Grace and John left after ten and their four followed an hour later. Lizzie went upstairs with the children and they all got ready for bed. Lizzie was surprised at how much she had missed them and hugged them tightly before tucking them up. They were delighted and surprised, it was a long time since she had done that.

Lizzie slept soundly until about one o'clock, when her mobile pinged. Groggily she reached for it and sleepy-eyed checked the number. Henry, she thought, could he not have waited until morning?

'Hi Henry, yes I arrived safely and was sound asleep until now,' she muttered angrily.

The deep breathing, so familiar started and now she was wide awake and sitting up in bed. She listened hard and could hear music in the background and muffled conversation. Was it a misdialled call, she wondered? She checked the number once again.

Now a woman's low voice was whispering, 'Oh I wish you could see how happy I make him!'

Then the call was ended, and Lizzie was left holding the phone and the tears started. They were tears of anger. As she lay down again, her peace shattered and bitter anger simmering in her heart. She had decided that she would not let 'That Woman' as she thought of her, upset her again. Why was she upset, did it not just prove that Henry was still having an affair with her? She lay still, staring at the ceiling and thought that divorce was now definitely on the cards. She would not put up with this nonsense any longer.

The next day they all went walking in the hills and if Lizzie was silent, nobody seemed to notice. The six children all chased each other around and gambolled happily, like young animals, as Anne remarked.

Grace later walked beside Lizzie and asked if all was well with her. She knew in her heart that Lizzie was troubled and had been told by Henry of the postnatal depression years ago. Grace was a strong practical woman and very discreet. She would not poke her nose into anybody's private business unless she was sure of herself. She and John had had a few shaky moments early on in their marriage, but that was ages ago and she felt that they were a good team.

Lizzie looked at her sister, ready to give the standard reply, 'Of course', but at the last second, she told her sister that she needed to speak to her at some time, alone and without anyone else present.

Grace had a moment's feeling of dismay. She suspected that it would not be good news.

The outing was a long one, lots of walking and climbing which wore out the children. Later when they were fed and in bed, Grace suggested going for a drive with Lizzie to the local pub. While there, she learned about Henry's affair and was shocked.

'Lizzie, are you absolutely sure about this? It really does not sound like Henry at all.' She shook her head and looked sadly at her younger sister.

Lizzie nodded, 'I know that you all think that I am the thorn in this marriage Grace, but it is not true. We barely speak anymore. I think I will have to get a divorce. These phone calls from his woman are driving me insane.'

She told Grace all about the phone calls and about her meeting with Linda Smythe and how Henry had told her of the affair, started before they married. How he swore the affair was over and how she did not believe him.

Grace was so shocked by these revelations that she honestly did not know what to say. Henry was one of the family and everyone loved him and respected him. To think that he was capable of this behaviour was mind-boggling. She agreed not to reveal any of this to the rest of the family. No point upsetting them all, Lizzie explained. The two women returned home subdued and sad.

Later that night, her phone rang again, and she checked the number. It was Henry. She wondered if she should bother answering it. It might not be him. She pressed the button and immediately heard Henry's voice. 'Lizzie, so sorry I did not ring earlier, you arrived safely I presume?'

Lizzie said dryly, 'Oh yes I arrived safely. Your phone woke me this morning at around one or two, but you probably know about that? Where were you?'

Henry thought quickly, did he ring her and when?

'No Lizzie, I don't think I rang you at all since you left, I feel bad about that, sorry. I was sort of busy all day after the trip home.' He waited for her answer but was already feeling queasy.

'Oh, I think you were very busy, Henry. I could hear the music and conversation. Sounded like a club or party. I hope you enjoyed yourselves.'

'Look Lizzie, I did not ring you. I went out with two of the doctors for a drink and then we decided to see what that new jazz club was like. It was only this morning I discovered that I had left my phone behind. I collected it around seven thirty tonight, when it opened.'

Before he could say anything else, Lizzie laughed and said, 'Right, and so it was not Linda's voice I heard speaking to me?'

Henry said hotly, 'Absolutely not, she was not at the club. I told you the truth Lizzie, but as usual you are accusing me wrongly.'

He finished the call there and then and decided that really, Lizzie was suffering from paranoia and that she was worse than he suspected.

The rest of the half term holiday dragged along for Lizzie. The children were so energetic and full of enthusiasm for activity and she felt drained. Grace was a great foil for their energy and organised outings that did not tire the adults so much. Anne was not up to too much walking and always opted to stay at home and prepare the meals instead. Lizzie joined her most of the time, and she knew Grace would understand. Finding it hard to fall asleep, she usually fell into a very deep sleep at dawn and then had trouble waking when the children were awake and noisily getting ready for breakfast. She wondered if she should get a stronger medication to cope. Not having alcohol really floored her and she was nervy and on edge the whole time.

On the day before they were due to leave, Henry suddenly made an appearance. Everyone was glad to see him but Lizzie. He breezed into the kitchen and greeted them all and explained that he had the weekend off and thought it would help if he drove the children home. He suggested that Lizzie might like to stay up there a while longer.

She looked at him coldly and asked, 'Are you capable of getting the children's school clothes ready?'

'I'm sure that our daughter is well able to sort out her uniform at this stage, aren't you Marianne?'

Marianne, used to the message system, nodded and said, 'Of course, I am, Dad.'

That night Henry went down to Grace and John's house and had a talk with them. Grace was left confused and upset. Henry's story seemed genuine and she felt that he was a genuinely nice and decent man. Between both stories, she did not know what to believe. She was being torn between two people whom she loved, and it was devastating her. It was like looking through a kaleidoscope and seeing two different patterns each time. Which one was the true and accurate one? John was no help and could not figure out what was happening, but took the male side, which was expected, Grace thought.

He said pompously, later when they were alone, 'Grace my dear, when illness occurs in the mind, truth is impossible to discern.'

Chapter 9

The last term of the year began. Nights were much darker now and the weather was cold and very wet. Lizzie hated this time of year. She met with her friends regularly and was invited to join them at the gym.

'It's really good for you, Lizzie and it does wonders for one's mental wellbeing too.' Kate and the other two nodded their heads and related how much the exercise had helped them, not just to get fit, but coping with growing children and their demands. Lizzie looked at them wondering just what they knew about her. It sounded to her as if they had been discussing her. Did they know about her mental problems?

Jenny said brightly, 'There is also a good badminton club at the gym, twice a week, aren't we very lucky with all the amenities that we have?'

Sarah asked Lizzie if she liked to play cards?

'Since I started playing bridge, I have met a whole bunch of new people and it's a great game.'

The other two said that they might consider playing bridge when they were ten years older, which caused much merriment.

Later that first week back to school, Lizzie had a visit from Viv. Delighted to see her friend, she made coffee and they sat in the conservatory, which was warm and cosy. Viv came straight to the point although Lizzie could see that she was a bit uncomfortable.

'Lizzie, you know that I respect and like you very much as my friend, but I have to also consider your wellbeing as my patient.' Lizzie nodded and wondered what was coming. She could nearly guess.

Viv told her that she suspected that she was not following her advice with the alcohol. When Lizzie remonstrated, Viv held up her hand and stopped her.

'I am not standing in judgement Lizzie, far be it from me to judge anybody, but I am worried, very worried. The consequences of mixing antidepressants and booze are very dangerous.' She sighed and looked over at Lizzie, who was staring out into the garden.

'So, what now? I thought it helped me, you know?' Lizzie bit her lip. She was not curious as to how Viv knew, but suspected Henry.

They talked about it for an hour and Lizzie told Viv that she would do whatever she suggested so long as the medication helped. Viv said that she was going to prescribe a new medication that was known to help long term postnatal depression and asked her to come into her surgery the next morning. Lizzie asked her if that meant she would always have to take medication? Viv confessed that she really did not know as everyone is different, but that she hoped not, and even if Lizzie needed it, there were many millions of people who were on permanent medication. At the end of the day, she argued, the important thing is feeling well and being able to cope with life. Lizzie had to agree with her.

So, Lizzie began her new regime and did not buy alcohol that term. She was determined to fight her demons. Her other 'demon' left her in peace. No more phone calls at all hours of the night. She and Henry discussed divorce. Henry was distraught and begged her to reconsider. He was so worried about the effect it would have on the children. He also felt dismayed about what his colleagues would think of him. He knew that he and his family were always considered a model family and was very proud of that status.

'Lizzie love, if you could see the heartbreak and confusion and guilt that children suffer from, as a result of parents splitting up, you would think twice. Please, think of the children, even if you don't love me anymore. I still love you. You know?'

Lizzie realised that all this was probably true, she loved her children too and didn't want them to suffer. About loving Henry, she was ambivalent. Too much had happened. Could she forgive and forget? She did not know the answer to that.

The following weeks leading up to Christmas were busy. The medication seemed to be working and she felt that she was coping. She reasoned to herself that after Christmas she would not need it anymore and felt happy that she was getting over her problem. Then just before the school broke up for the holiday, the phone calls started again. This time is was when the children had just gone to school and Lizzie was at home. The landline would ring and when she picked it up the same breathing and horrible messages would come out.

'Did she know what her husband was up to? Did she trust him? Did she know that he wanted to replace her?'

On and on it went. Now, she refused to answer the phone and as a result, her friends started to call in on her, not being able to get through to her, either on her mobile or landline.

She warned Ivy not to answer the phone and told her there were a lot of scam calls coming through.

One day Jenny called to the house and wondered what on earth was wrong.

'Kate was so upset. She could not reach you and her little one was taken ill at school and she was up country visiting her sick mother. I would have gone in and taken her home, but I was at work and didn't get the message until later. All the girls work you know, so you were her only hope.'

'I'm so sorry Jenny, I didn't know. I keep getting annoying calls, so I have stopped answering my phone.' She smiled apologetically and spread her hands.

Jenny could not believe her ears. Wait until the girls heard this!

'What if it was your Marianne or Mark, Lizzie, who would they call? In the end they had to keep her in sick bay in the boarding part of the school, which was not ideal.'

Lizzie shook her head, 'I am really sorry Jenny. Please explain to the girls, will you?'

She realised that she would have to be ready to answer the phones, like it or not. As Jenny had pointed out, it could have been one of her children that needed help. She wondered how she would get over Christmas without her daily drink and bought some as a backup, just in case, she told herself.

Mark and Marianne played sport regularly at the new sports facility a mile away and it was while waiting for them one night, that she saw Linda coming out of the nearby gym. She watched to see which way she went and was surprised to see her walking with her sports bag, she disappeared out of view, and Lizzie reached the conclusion that she must live in the vicinity if she didn't need her car. It was on one such night, while waiting for her children to finish their activities, that she decided to follow Linda and see where she lived.

It became routine. Now that she knew where That Woman lived, she felt in control of her feelings and a sense of power accompanied that. The woman was always alone, and the house seemed empty until she entered and switched on the lights inside. It was an old three-story red brick house in a settled area. Everything about the street was clean and well kept. The gardens all looked professionally cared for and the cars parked outside each house were not very old models, mostly the cars were parked in the driveways of these houses.

It became quite enjoyable, this following of Linda who was oblivious to the fact that the same car slowly followed her from the gym every Tuesday evening. Some nights Lizzie would walk a little way behind her, it was only about a mile and a half. Lizzie would smile to herself and wonder what Henry would think of her stalking the woman. At least she would now know where to look for his car, when he rang home to say he would be late.

Christmas holidays came and they were staying at home this year. The weather forecast was not good for travelling anyway. On Christmas Eve, Henry got a telephone call from his mother to say that his father had just had a slight turn and was admitted to hospital. Of course, he had to go and visit him and give his mother his support. They all usually went there for the New Year celebrations. The children of course wanted to go and see their grandad, but Henry said that as he was in hospital, it would be better to wait until they got the all clear. Besides, what about their Christmas presents? Henry advised them to wait and see how grandad was and when he would be coming home, they still might be going there for New Year.

That night it started to snow, and the children forgot all about their disappointment at not going with their Dad. They all went to church on Christmas morning and met with their neighbours and friends. Tea and cakes were served afterwards in the church hall, every mother contributing a plate of food. It was a quick social gathering as all the children were anxious to return to their presents.

The days following Christmas were dreamlike. The snow was quite thick on the ground and every child, it seemed, went to the park with sledges and screamed in delight as they slid down the various hills there. It was a big woodland area where normally they would bring their bikes for the woodland trails, or skateboards for the designated area. All three were well wrapped up and Lizzie enjoyed walking in the cold crisp air. She trailed through the woods as the children played with their friends on their sledges. As she strode along, she came to the boundary of the park and realised for the first time, that it bordered the area where Linda lived. In fact, the north gate to the park was almost opposite the house where she lived. Looking at the house she saw no signs of life there. She guessed that Linda must be away for the holiday. No car was parked in the drive either. Well, she thought, how easy it was, to keep an eye on her enemy!

Henry was on his way home. His father had suffered a mild heart attack and was back at home resting. His mother felt that it would be better if she kept him quiet for a few weeks until his next check-up, so Henry promised that the Easter holidays would be a good time to visit with the children and the weather would be better too, hopefully.

Marianne and Mark were delighted to see their father back and showed him all the presents they had received. They were relieved that their grandad was alright and were appreciative of the gifts of money that granny sent them.

Over the next few days there were some parties to attend at neighbouring houses, annual events that different people hosted. Kate was hosting one tonight, and the children were excited as it meant a late night. Lizzie was tired but determined to keep up appearances. She even made the effort to go out early and have her hair trimmed and coloured. She met Jenny as she came out of the salon and the two decided to go for coffee. They managed to find a space for two in their favourite meeting place in town. Jenny had been shopping in the sales and bought some items which she was excited about. Lizzie realised that she could really do with a few new clothes and the two chatted about which was the best place for bargains. As they left the cafe and got caught up again in the milling crowds on the pavement, Jenny shouted, 'See you tonight Lizzie,' and disappeared into the throng.

Lizzie looked at the crowded street and the busy shops and decided to head out to a quieter shopping area. She drove out of town and parked her car. Shopping was usually a chore, but she really needed a few tops. She went to a boutique known to her and found what she was looking for. Delighted with herself, she headed back to her car. As she put her bags into the boot, she heard someone say her name and looked up. There was Linda looking very glamorous in a short fur jacket and high boots. Lizzie did not greet her as she closed the door, but as Linda was standing in her way, she had to look at her.

'Seasons' greetings, Liz, I hope you had a wonderful Christmas.' She smiled broadly at Lizzie.

'Yes, thank you, we did,' Lizzie said stiffly and moved towards the driver's door.

Linda stepped aside and said, 'I expect Henry has told you how we are amalgamating and will hopefully be working side by side very soon?' She looked at Lizzie questioningly. 'It makes a lot of sense to keep our two departments under one umbrella, don't you think? Anyway, I'm sure Henry has told you about our meeting and conversation.'

Lizzie still did not answer but just opened the door and got in slowly and gently as though she did not see or hear Linda.

Driving home, she turned the news over in her head. So that's how things were developing. Now they would have a working partnership and there would be no need for excuses. They would see each other continually. Lizzie wondered why she did not feel surprised by the news. Well, it would not affect her, she thought, I will not think about it. Maybe now she will cease telephoning me. She can no longer touch me. Lizzie tried to pretend that she did not care, but deep in her heart and mind she knew that the anger would never go away. She would have to find a way to cope with it.

Chapter 10

The party at Kate and Michael's house was a noisy affair and all the kids were in another room where the disco music was blaring. After a couple of hours, Lizzie's head was aching. Searching for Kate she apologised and said that she had to leave, she did not feel well and no, please don't tell Henry and spoil his evening, she would just slip out quietly. Kate commiserated with her but understood.

As she left herself into the house, the phone was ringing. As she picked it up, she hoped Henry's father was alright. The usual breathing started, then glasses tinkling and the hated lowered voice. She did not wait to hear the message but slammed down the phone. How had That Woman known that she was alone in the house? She felt the old anger building up inside her and the feeling of being violated in her own home. Going upstairs to her room, she searched in her wardrobe for the bottle of vodka and sat on the bed drinking.

At twelve she heard the front door open and she hurriedly got into bed and put the bottle under her pillow. When Henry put his head around the door to see if she was alright, she pretended to be asleep. She could hear the children grumble about having to leave the party while it was still going on and Henry saying how late it was and that there would be another party in two days' time to attend. That seemed to quieten them, and the house descended into silence.

She awoke at some stage, struggling to breathe, someone was on top of her pressing down on her head. She struggled and kicked out and could only hear her muffled screams. Her heart was pounding as she tried to get her breath and then with her last remaining strength she pushed and kicked and felt herself falling, falling. She opened her eyes. She was lying on the floor and her legs were entangled with the top sheet. Her duvet was clenched tightly in her hand and her pillow lying on her chest. Gasping, she looked around for her attacker. There was nobody in the room. Her body was drenched in sweat and she thought her heart would burst, it was pounding so much. Eventually, she found the strength to crawl out of the tangled sheet and duvet, and onto her knees. She reached for her bedside light and switched it on. Looking around, everything seemed normal, there was no sound at all. Her door was shut as it had been. She suddenly realised that she had been dreaming. She sat on the unmade bed and tried to understand that it must have been a dream. After some time, she pulled the sheet back onto the bed and the rest of the bedclothes and climbed in. She lay with her eyes open, staring at the ceiling and tried to focus. She remembered the vodka and looked around for the bottle. There is was, at the headboard, empty. Could she really have drunk the whole bottle? Surely not! Eventually she fell into a doze, with the light still on.

The next couple of days the children were bored as the snow had melted and they wanted to go out and play. Lizzie was unable to think straight and told them to ask their father to bring them. She returned to bed whenever she could and slept easily, but she never felt as though she had had enough sleep. Tiredness and lethargy were all she experienced. She rang Kate the day after the dream and asked if she could possibly take the two children to play with hers. She knew that she was not being fair as Kate had hosted a large party. Kate agreed to come and collect them. They would be going ice skating later. She did not comment on how Lizzie looked; haggard and drawn with bloodshot eyes. She confided to Jenny later that she thought that Lizzie was still drinking.

Henry came home from work and showered. There was a smaller party tonight, held in the church hall for whoever was free to come. It was New Year's Eve and generally this was regarded as a party for the children and was over by nine, after which, most of the parents went out celebrating. The pizza was all supplied by the parish committee and the mothers had a well-earned rest. Lizzie was sitting in her dressing gown when Henry came into the sitting room.

'For heaven's sake, Lizzie, can't you get yourself ready? We need to be there in forty minutes.'

She turned blank eyes towards him and shook her head. 'I don't think I'm up to it Henry, can't you take the children by yourself?'

'No, this is a community event, what on earth will people think? You cannot even make the effort to appear for two hours? It only happens once a year, for God's sake. Pull yourself together woman.'

He strode out of the room angrily and shouted to the children that he hoped that they were ready to go. Lizzie rose wearily and went upstairs to dress herself. She would do it, just to show that man that she was well capable of putting on a show, like he did.

The children enjoyed themselves. Games had been organised. They all received a small party bag of treats. The pizza had disappeared quickly and now they were all going home to bed.

Henry told Lizzie that he had to attend a get-together with his colleagues at a local hotel and that she was welcome to come as all the wives and girlfriends would probably be there. He noticed her pallor and felt a momentary pity for her.

He said gently, 'Lizzie, you don't have to come to this if you don't feel like it. I know that you are tired, but it's up to you.'

She shook her head and walked up the stairs to her room. He watched her go and his face settled into the now habitual look of unhappiness.

When she heard his car leave. She went to check on the children. They were fast asleep in their rooms. Going downstairs carefully, she got her purse from her bag and quietly let herself out the front door. There was an off-licence nearby and surely it would still be open. It was, and she purchased two bottles of vodka and was back home in twenty minutes. She knew that she must not overdo it like the last time and put one bottle under the kitchen sink and climbed the stairs to her bedroom with the other one.

She had barely started to sip her drink when the phone rang. She did not want the children to be wakened and ran down to the hall phone, she had stopped having a landline phone in her room months earlier. There it began again, the breathing, glasses tinkling. Now she could hear Henry's voice clearly in the background. Talking medicine as usual, "diagnostics" this and "patterns" that, then it faded, and she heard the woman whisper, 'See, I have him where I want him, with me'. The call ended, and Lizzie stared at the receiver in her hand. As usual there was no caller number showing. She left the phone off the hook and went back upstairs.

Later, she was in a darkened room and she could hear voices arguing. She was trying to protect herself against the voices and was hitting out as hard as she could. She would kill those voices once and for all. She could see her hands, even though it was quite dark. They were wet and looking closely she could see they were covered in blood. Gasping she jumped up and knew she must clean her hands before anyone saw them. Then she woke up. Of course, there was no blood on her hands, and she felt foolish standing in the middle of her bedroom looking at her hands. She looked for the bottle of vodka and found it standing on the floor beside her bed, where she had left it. She examined it fearfully to see how much she had drunk and was pleased to see that there was more than three quarters there, so she knew that she had not been drunk.

From then on, when Henry was at work or out anywhere at night, as soon as the children were in bed, she would take the phone off the hook. It was her enemy.

Bad dreams continued to haunt Lizzie and she knew that she needed help but who could she go to? Henry would ask her if she was drinking and had warned her that she might have to go away for rehabilitation to one of these fancy clinics. No way was she going to be put out of her house.

She made an appointment with Viv and explained about the difficulty in sleeping. She did not mention the dreams and the voices tormenting her or the phone calls. At this stage, she felt that Viv was a little sceptical about her, although very understanding and friendly. She swore that she was not drinking. She felt relieved and confident having sleeping tablets prescribed to her.

She slept as much as possible during the day while the children were at school, as the night time was the worst, never knowing when the phone would ring, if it would ring, or if the dreams would come. Henry had come back one night and found the phone off the hook. He was very angry with her.

'What if my mother is trying to get through to me?' he shouted. He was worried about his father and knew that the man was not well. He usually rang his mother from his hospital office every morning around eleven to enquire about his father's health and always told her to ring him any time of day or night and he would come to her.

School started again, and the children settled into their routine. Ivy came each morning and helped them get ready and got their lunch boxes ready if Lizzie was not up and about. The dreams were becoming nightly horrors for Lizzie and she knew she could not keep going at this rate. She was very fearful that she was losing her mind and that Henry would have her committed to an institution. If that happened, would she ever be freed again?

Ivy could see that Lizzie was troubled and asked her outright one morning. At first, Lizzie brushed her concern aside, but then feeling so tired and worn out, she told Ivy about her postnatal depression and how it was becoming permanent. Ivy listened to it all in silence and without interrupting once. When Lizzie finally ran out of words, Ivy nodded her head and told her that she as a mother, knew all about it. Her own daughter had suffered the same way. After years of therapy she was now finally cured. She had also used alcohol for a time, her marriage had broken up and eventually, she went to a special unit that looked after depressed people, particularly women. Now she was living alone with her three children and Ivy helped her out, babysitting when needed and kept an eye on her. Ivy was convinced that her daughter was now cured. She told Lizzie to seek what help she needed and not to be afraid to try a clinic or whatever was needed to get her life back on track. It was such a relief for Lizzie to be able to talk to someone who she felt understood her problem.

She did not of course confide in Ivy about the telephone calls. That was too personal, and she knew that she would have been shocked if one of her friends had told her anything like that.

She began to deal with the telephone calls when Henry was out, by picking up the phone, saying nothing and replacing it when she heard the familiar breathing. What a pity Henry was never there to take these calls, she often thought. But then, he probably knew the caller and it would turn into an ordinary conversation, she supposed.

A feeling of anger was growing in her and a desire to inflict terrible injury on the person responsible. She never did have a bad temper, now she felt that she was changing, and that she could become violent. That frightened her too. Was it yet another sign that she was losing her mind?

When football practice resumed in early in January, she began to watch out for Linda Smythe. Sure enough, her routine did not seem to change. As before, on Tuesday night at seven thirty, she could be seen walking or sometimes jogging the distance home from the gym to her house, in her track suit and backpack. She must go home straight from work, change and then go to the gym, Lizzie guessed. An idea began to form in her mind. At first it was just like a daydream. Then as the days went by, details started to become part of the idea and soon her brain had worked out a plot to get her revenge. Would she have the courage she wondered and guessed that she would not.

Then there was another call. This time on her mobile when she was in bed. She did not know whether Henry was back and in bed, as she had been asleep. She looked at her clock. It was two o'clock. She decided to answer silently. Again, the pause, the whispered message was this time without the usual background noise. An invitation to come and see her and let her explain why she was making such a nuisance of herself, a chance to redeem herself, she whispered. 'You know where I live, Liz. I have observed you watching, you see. So why not come and beard the old witch in her den? Next Tuesday and I shall reveal all my dear.'

Click, the phone went dead, and Lizzie stared at it dumbfounded. What now, she wondered? Did she want to apologise for her behaviour? Lizzie lay down, puzzled and wide awake. She had a few days to consider what she would do.

Chapter 11

Henry was busy after the Christmas break. As soon as school restarted the days flew by for him. He also wanted to start up little meetings with various parents as a sort of group support for them. After all, they were all struggling with the demands on their lives with difficult children. The parents welcomed such meetings and he encouraged them to start up the gatherings once a month or so in their own homes, taking turns to hold them. He wanted this to be away from the hospital setting and make it more a community effort between the parents, a place where they could chat and compare notes. He felt quite excited at the progress being made.

Lizzie was on edge all the week leading up to the Tuesday. She wondered if she had imagined the phone call at times. Things were often like that these days. Some things that were not real at all, appeared real, and some things that happened, she dismissed as imaginary. Like Marianne's piano lesson, missed yesterday because she thought that she had already had it. Marianne tearfully told her that her lesson had been the previous week and now she had missed this week. She was so upset as she really loved her music lessons and played her digital piano, upstairs in her bedroom, for hours on end. Lizzie had been so remorseful and arranged with Marianne to keep a calendar on the kitchen wall with dates and activities printed on it and that every day, they would all check it.

She barely slept over the weekend thinking about Tuesday night. Was it Tuesday night? She suddenly panicked, could she have got it wrong? She tossed and turned on Monday night, her head aching and her heart pounding. At three o'clock in the morning, her mobile phone pinged. She leapt up, to answer it and again came the whispered,

'Liz, just to remind you, we meet tonight, remember? I will leave the door open for you, come around eight as I must shower after the gym, alright?' The caller finished without waiting for a reply.

Wednesday was a free day due to teacher training, so the children would have no school. When Marianne asked tentatively if she could sleep over at her friend Jane's house, she was surprised and delighted when her mother agreed. Usually it was a negative answer. Neither parent liked sleepovers and they always refused requests. Mark was highly indignant and immediately rang his pal Tommy and asked if he could sleep over. Thirty minutes later he arrived in the kitchen grinning. After football, he was going with Tommy for a pizza and sleepover, he announced. Lizzie looked at him blankly, hardly hearing what he said. She then realised that she would be totally free and could go to her meeting without having to worry about the children. She arranged to drop the children to their friends with their night things and sportswear as all the children involved would be at sports training together that night. Henry would be late as usual she presumed.

   She dressed carefully. Her plan, hatched in the depths of her misery, was finally coming together. She sat down and tried to think calmly about the route she would take after leaving the house. She was going to walk to the park and watch for Linda's arrival. Going into Henry's bedroom she opened his wardrobe and searched for what she wanted. Satisfied, she took a sports bag and left her mobile phone in her bedroom. She put on her trainers and she looked in the mirror. She looked as though she was on her way to the gym.

   Standing outside the gate of the park, across the road from Linda's house, she watched and waited. Just before seven thirty, the now familiar figure jogged up the road and turned into her house, running up the steps lightly, to the front door. She waited for the usual lights to go on and looked at her watch. Right, she would now be in the shower. Lizzie felt she might be conspicuous standing still for another thirty minutes, so she started walking up the road that Linda had just jogged down. She suddenly felt nervous, her heart was fluttering, and she felt perspiration running down her back between her shoulder blades. She walked slowly without any hurry and did not see anybody. It had started raining quite

heavily and she was glad she had on her hooded jacket that she always wore walking. At seven fifty-nine, she retraced her steps and looked around her carefully as she turned into the drive of Linda's house. Not a soul was to be seen in the driving rain. She ran up the steps and paused by the door. Putting her hand on it gently, she found it was indeed unlatched and she quietly entered. She stood silently in the hall, 'Hello,' she called uncertainly.
There was no sound at all, but a little light was showing from under the door of the front room, on her right. Gingerly, she stepped softly to the door and pushed it open.

  Henry was hoping for an early night. It had been very busy, and the department of health people were also trying to get another meeting arranged. They had not given up on the plan to amalgamate the services and he was fearful that they would get their way in the end. At six thirty his mobile rang. It was his mother weeping. His father had just had another heart attack and was in the ambulance now, going to the hospital. She felt it was more serious this time. Henry assured her that he was on his way. He rang home to tell Lizzie but there was no answer. She must be out with the children. He would ring again on his way to his mother. It would take him the best part of two hours to get there and he prayed he would be on time. He knew it would be serious. The cardiologist had warned them that a second one might mean the end. The man had serious heart problems. He alerted the staff nurse and asked if she would contact the manager and let him know where he was going.

Lizzie reached home, soaked to the skin. She was exhilarated but still in shock and could not stop shaking. She entered the hall and immediately went upstairs and ran a bath. Stripping all her clothes off she got into the hot water and lay immobile, her mind racing. She stayed in the bath until she realised she was cold. She then hurriedly dried herself and put on her night clothes. Feverishly she gathered her discarded clothes and crept down the stairs to the utility room. She pushed the clothes into the washing machine, everything, including her shoes and jacket and turned on a cold wash. Then she emptied the bag, took up the knife from the floor and looked at it blankly. Returning upstairs she put the knife at the back of her wardrobe and found her vodka. As she dried her hair, she looked at the clock. Only nine thirty. She could hardly believe it. She must have walked back very fast indeed. Had she run? She could not remember. Her mind was blank. She had to be in bed before Henry came back. She finished her drink and returned to the utility room. The washing machine was silent, it's cycle, over. She then put in more detergent and turned the machine onto a hot cycle and retraced her steps up to her bedroom and the vodka bottle. Then she remembered the phone and went down to replace the receiver. She would not have to worry about any more mystery phone calls. She giggled as she went upstairs.

The phone was ringing, and she could not surface from the deep sleep she was in. Fumbling with her duvet she hauled herself out of bed and went down to the hall. She mumbled 'Hello', her brain trying to unravel who it was. Then she remembered the children and shouted, 'Hello, who is that?' She heard Henry's voice from far away. There was a lot of crackling and she could not understand what he was saying. She could hear a storm raging outside, and thunder was crashing. She could not hear his voice. She put down the phone in frustration. She stood looking down at the phone and wondering what he was ringing her for. What time was it? She peered at her watch. Midnight for heaven's sake, why was he this late she wondered? As she returned to her bedroom, the phone rang again, and she retraced her steps. This time the line was clearer. It was Henry again.

'Where on earth have you been? I've been trying to reach you since seven o'clock. Dad had a massive heart attack and has sadly passed away just an hour ago. I'm here with Mum and going to take her home now.' He paused for breath and Lizzie tried to gather her senses and reply.

'I'm so sorry Henry, what should I do? What do you want me to do?'

Henry replied, 'Look, I'll ring you first thing in the morning and tell you what to bring up. The children will need their decent clothes. The funeral will probably be on Thursday. Talk to you soon, must bring Mum home now, and Betts. They are both very upset, as you can imagine.'

Lizzie would never recall driving the next day to her in-law's house. She vaguely remembered Henry's hurried phone call that morning. He wanted her to bring his navy suit and a couple of good shirts and a navy tie and his good shoes and socks. She tried to write it all down after he finished, frightened that she would forget something. She rang her friends and explained what had happened and they, full of sympathy, dropped the children home after breakfast. She was not to worry, they insisted. They would explain to their teachers what had happened, and she must take her time and not rush back straight after the funeral.

Jenny and Kate met afterwards that day and said how shocked they had been at Lizzie's appearance. The news must have shocked her badly they agreed, to look like that.

Lizzie tried to be as calm as she could on meeting Henry's mother and Betts. There were many callers and Lizzie kept to the kitchen as much as possible, making tea and coffee and washing teacups. The next day was the same. She stood beside Henry as many people filed past them in the church, shaking hands and offering their condolences. Lizzie said nothing, just nodded. She was holding herself together by tightening up everything inside her and standing as still as a statue. If she relaxed, she was afraid that she would fall in a heap on the floor. The children, although sad, were composed and serious and Henry was very proud of them. The funeral was short and over quickly. The mist and drizzle made it a very depressing occasion.

That evening, after all the callers had departed, the family sat together in the sitting room, trying to rest and talk normally, but it was a tense situation. Lizzie was relieved when Henry suggested an early night for them all. She shepherded the children to bed after they had cuddled their grandmother. Sitting in the dark, when they were asleep, she struggled to find a restful place for her mind, which was in turmoil. Was this all happening, or was it all a bad dream? Was she going to wake up and find herself at home in her own bed? She opened the bottle of vodka she had brought in her bag and drank it straight from the bottle. She could not bear to go down and find a glass and maybe bump into one of them. At some stage she fell asleep.

In the coming days, Henry had things to check over with his mother and Betts and the solicitor. His father, being a businessman had left his affairs and everything in order and there was not a lot of paperwork to do, or decisions to be made. Betts was more upset than her mother and Henry felt that they both needed a little sedation and lots of rest. He suggested a walk later in the afternoon, the weather was quite mild for this time of year and his mother was happy to go with him. The children and Betts also went but Lizzie pleaded a headache and lack of sleep. She desperately wanted to see the news on the television. As soon as they were gone, she sat down and scanned all the news channels. There was nothing much to be seen, no mention of anyone being murdered. She went through all the channels again, in a panic. Nothing! She turned off the television and sat wringing her hands and staring at the blank screen. What day was it? Friday? Surely there would be some mention of a murder in their town?

That evening while Henry made some phone calls. The children and Lizzie were in the sitting room. The children were playing games on their iPods and the television was on low while Lizzie waited impatiently for the news to come on. Henry's mother was resting in her room and Betts was in the kitchen, finding solace apparently, in baking.

Mark looked up and said, 'Mum, Tommy's mum had number five last week, you know?'

Lizzie, eyes glued on the screen said, 'What's that, Mark?'

Mark rolled his eyes and said, 'Tommy has another sister, "Number Four" he's calling her. He's fed up with four sisters. One is bad, can you imagine four?'

Marianne lifted her head and retorted, 'I wouldn't mind another sister, one brother is more than enough!'

Mark looked at Lizzie and said, 'Why did you stop Mum, I would have liked a brother to play with. That would be cool.'

Lizzie did not reply, so intent was she at catching any news that might come on. Henry came back into the room with a newspaper and sat down beside the fire. He smiled at the children and began reading.

Mark was still thinking about his friend.

'How is it Dad, that some ladies cannot have children at all, and other ladies can't stop having them?' Henry looked at his son in surprise.

Mark explained about Tommy's newest sister, "Number Four". 'He is hoping his Mum might have four more, all boys,' he explained. 'Mum has stopped so I will never have a brother I suppose, and Viv cannot have babies at all, just imagine that!' He looked at his father as though for an explanation.

Henry looked at his son in astonishment. 'How on earth do you know that about Viv?'

'I asked her,' he replied with a cheeky grin. 'When we went ice skating that time, 'cos she is so good with children. I think that she would be a cool Mum,' he said with that heartbreaking wisdom that children sometimes show.

Lizzie listened puzzled to their conversation and then her attention became focused on the news. She reached for the remote and turned up the volume. Henry had never known her to be interested in the news and was looking at her. Mark still wanted to chatter but his mother shushed him.

'Quiet Mark, I want to hear the news.'

They returned home a week after the funeral. Henry had left the day before them, to be back at work as soon as possible. The children were silent for the journey, engrossed in their iPods. Every hour Lizzie switched the radio to the news channel. There was no news to interest her at all.

Was it all imagination then, had nothing happened? She puzzled over it as she drove. How did she reach this stage in her life, that she could not remember what she did or was not sure of what she did any more? Was it the medication she was taking? It made life unreal, somehow. There were days, she knew, that she could hardly remember anything about. If she was asked what she did yesterday, she would have trouble remembering. Was she always like that? She worried that she was losing her mind. It happened, didn't it, to people? Who could she talk to about it? Her friends would not understand, just like Henry and Viv. She imaged a conversation with Jenny and Kate; 'Girls, you know I think I'm losing my mind, I feel desperate, can you help me, please?' They would look at her and run, or worse, pat her on the back and say that they all felt like that, somedays. They would never look at her the same way again and she would have lost her friends and have no one.

On reaching home she immediately put on the television to the news channel. When Henry came home later that night, he found his wife sitting silently watching, with such intense concentration, that he wondered what on earth her new interest was about. He had never known Lizzie to be very interested in the shows on television and certainly not the news. He asked her what she was so interested in and received no answer. He went to the kitchen to make himself a drink and when he returned, she had gone upstairs, to bed, he assumed.

Chapter 12

It was in the last week of January, on a Thursday, that the news of Professor Smythe's murder broke. People had been asking about her all that week as she was due back from holidays the weekend before. Because she had missed many appointments both at the university and the hospital, people started getting anxious. Eventually the police were contacted when a friend called by the house and found the dreadful scene. She had been savagely stabbed to death and had seemed to be taken unawares. She was in her gym clothing and an interrupted burglary was suspected. The gym was able to give them the information that her last visit had been the second Tuesday in January. The strange addition to the scene was a man's tie around the victim's neck, tied in a bow. Now the police were beginning to delve into the investigation. The murder weapon was being searched for, and the park area was cordoned off as officers searched the area, yard by yard. It was all over the news and everyone was talking about it. Nothing as shocking had ever happened in the neighbourhood before. Her colleagues in the hospital and university were asked to be available to be interviewed about their knowledge of the dead woman.

Henry was shocked as were all his colleagues. Not many of the doctors liked Linda actually, she was a law unto herself and could be intimidating. She used her position to get the results that she wanted. Still, nobody would have wished for such an end to the unfortunate professor.

Lizzie retreated into herself and stopped looking at the news. She avoided being alone with Henry but there was suddenly a feeling of relaxation in the house. She was found one day by her children out in the garden, staring into space. When Marianne asked her what she was doing, she replied that she was visualising the garden in summer and on that occasion broke out into giggles.

Grace and the children visited Lizzie in February for midterm break. She was shocked by Lizzie's deterioration. The children as usual noticed nothing. Grace spoke with Henry the first night there, after Lizzie went to bed, as she did most nights with the children. She began hesitantly at first and apologised to Henry for not having had this chat much earlier. Henry poured them both a glass of wine and told her to go on, he was sure that she had nothing to apologise about.

Grace told him about her mother. She had also suffered postnatal depression she thought. It was such a long time ago and as children they had not understood anything really. When they were in their teens, her father had explained all about their mother's death. She had been so lively for years, but after Lizzie's birth, had gone downhill very quickly. In those days it was hardly recognised as a serious condition and the doctor had thought that the woman just needed a holiday and a good rest. Farming was not an easy life for a woman in those parts. Their father had felt guilty afterwards about his wife's death and wished that he had understood better, the illness that she must have suffered.

Henry interrupted Grace to ask how her mother had died. Grace took a sip of her drink and hesitated. 'She hanged herself out in the barn one night, and my Dad found her the next morning.'

Henry digested this information in silence for a time and then asked, 'Does Lizzie know about her mother's death?'

Grace said it was understood from their teenage years that Lizzie was never to be told, in case the child blamed herself for her mother's death.

He shook his head sadly. 'Grace, I should have been told this after the first sign of depression. This explains an awful lot, you know. As of now, she is borderline psychotic, and will need hospitalising shortly, I think.'

Grace agreed and apologised again. Every member of the family had decided that Lizzie must never get a hint about the death her mother had. Seeing how happy she was when she married Henry, they had hoped that the same problem would not affect her. Grace had not suffered from postnatal depression, and nobody else in the family had psychiatric problems. How were they expected to know it would strike again? After Lizzie had Marianne, Grace had spoken to her father about it and tried to jog his memory about when and how her mother had been when she first started acting strangely. Of course, the elderly man could not quite remember now. Life was always busy on the farm and it was work, work, work, day in and day out, seven days a week, fifty-two weeks a year. He could remember Christmases best because there was a bit of time to relax then. He could recall clearly, the day he found his wife going out to the barn to feed the chickens at eleven o'clock one night, and he followed her, telling her that she had fed them that day and it was night time now and the wrong time. She had just looked at him blankly and went back with him to the house. As far as he would remember, that was the first time that he felt there was something amiss with his wife.

Henry refilled their glasses and sat down again. 'I really don't know where to begin Grace. I know that my wife has been unhappy for a long time and that she thinks I am the cause of her misery. How can I fix that? I never witnessed any of the strange phone calls, she says she gets, or got any myself so I just don't know.'

'Maybe they were all in her imagination, Henry? She has just got obsessed with this other woman, hasn't she? She is the one that was murdered, isn't she?'

Henry nodded his head. 'Yes, if she had done that to poor Lizzie, I would say that it served her right. But that is an awful thing to say, isn't it? The woman was a menace in more ways than one. She tortured me and many other young students I dare say. A sinister, manipulative person. I wonder what *her* mental health was like. I expect that quite a few people are glad that she is not around anymore.'

Grace rose to leave for bed. 'Should I have a word with her and explain what is happening to her, Henry?'

He rose too and picked up the glasses, stopping to think about that.

'I think that at this stage, play it by ear, try to put her at ease and make her laugh and be happy. She may talk to you about her fears of going away for treatment.'

The children all went ice skating the next day and Grace and Lizzie sat watching them and drinking coffee. Grace gently asked Lizzie how she was feeling?

Lizzie smiled at her and said, 'Never better, Grace. My problems are over, I think. Must just cut down on the alcohol. It's not good with medicine, is it?' She dissolved into giggles and Grace felt a bit alarmed. But then, normal conversation resumed, and she seemed quite rational. They met Viv at the rink. She had two young pre-teens in tow. She sat down with the two ladies and gave the teens some money for chips. She explained, she was giving their mother a break from them. The teenagers were patients of hers and were lovely kids if just a bit messed up. Grace and Viv had met years ago and had a lot to talk about. Lizzie drifted off into a reverie.

Grace returned home five days later to prepare for her children's return to school. Marianne and Mark also got their school bags ready and were looking forward to going back. Grace had made Lizzie promise to come for the Easter holidays and said they would have a nice restful time with lots of fresh air. Lizzie nodded and smiled and said that she would like that.

After sports activities the following week, Henry was at his clinic and Lizzie felt for the first time, pleasantly tired and looked forward to a good night's rest. For the past couple of weeks, she felt that she was in a dream, but a pleasant one this time. She could not help smiling to herself now and again and thinking that her life was back to what it used to be.

As she passed the phone on her way to bed, it rang. She picked up the receiver, and before she had time to say hello, she stopped still as the usual deep breathing started and she listened in horror to the hated voice.

'Liz.' This time it was almost sung, like 'Li-iz.' She nearly dropped the phone. The voice went on, 'I'm still here though, aren't I?'

Then it was over. Lizzie stared in horror at the phone. It cannot be, she thought. She is not here anymore, she's dead!

She hurried up the stairs and reached the safety of her bedroom and threw herself on the bed. She felt like screaming. She was silently screaming inside herself. How could a dead woman still reach her, it was not possible. She went to her locker and took out her vodka and took several quick gulps. She sat in the dark room, hardly daring to breathe.

She heard Henry come in later and go into the kitchen and later still, into the sitting room. She could hear the television on low and guessed he would be watching the news. She dressed for bed and lay as still as a statue under the covers, her mind whirling about. She did not imagine this, she did not. Or, did she? Did it really happen? Eventually she slept.

Her door opened, and she watched as Linda floated into the room. She was grinning maniacally and twirling Henry's tie around in the air, like a ribbon. Then she drifted over and stood above Lizzie and her grin changed to a dreadful grimace and blood came out of her mouth and was falling on Lizzie.

'No, no, no', Lizzie screamed as loudly as she could, 'Leave me alone, you're dead, go away.'

Her screaming woke up Henry and the children. He dashed into his wife's room and beheld the apparition of his wife, kneeling on her bed, wailing and pulling at her hair. He threw his arms around her and was amazed at her strength as she pushed him away. He nearly fell. He stepped forward again and put his arms firmly around Lizzie.

'Wake up, Lizzie, it's only a dream.'

Gradually she quietened and stayed very still. 'Henry, am I covered in her blood? Is there blood on my arms, look, please?'

He put on the bedside light and looked at her arms. 'No, of course there is no blood, it was a nightmare, Liz.'

She didn't believe him and had to look herself and then dragged herself off the bed and went into the bathroom and closed the door. Henry could hear the shower running. He went out and closed the bedroom door and assured his terrified children who were standing at their bedroom door, clutching each other, that Mum only had a nightmare. He tried to smile at them.

'Not only children have night terrors, you know. Now let's all go back to bed again. He brought them back to their beds and tucked them in and then went back to his own.

As he lay gazing up at the ceiling, he wondered what her mind could be imagining. Could medication cure his wife? He would contact Viv first thing in the morning and ask her opinion and find out how soon could an admission to the clinic be arranged. He knew that things had gone on for too long and felt no more time could be wasted. He thought about his children and what effect it might have on them. Would he be able to manage them alone, with Ivy's help? They were too young for boarding school. To uproot them from their school and friends and send them up to Grace might be more detrimental to their wellbeing. Whatever about the children, he knew that something had to be done for Lizzie now, before she deteriorated further.

How he wished with all his heart that he had done something sooner to help her. It was dawn before he fell into a fitful sleep.

Chapter 13

At breakfast the next morning, Henry had a long conversation with Ivy, who listened without interrupting him. She understood the problem and told Henry she would be available as long and whenever he needed her, to look after the children. He left early to go to meet Viv, before his days' work began. She agreed to talk to Lizzie as soon as possible that day.

Viv rang Lizzie at ten o'clock to ask her to come in to see her, but Ivy explained that Lizzie was still in bed. Viv asked her to give Lizzie the message as soon as she was up and about.

Lizzie felt hung over and exhausted. She didn't remember the nightmare but felt that something had snapped in her and that Henry was involved somehow. She was delighted to hear that Viv had rung and would see her. She knew that she needed something powerful to straighten her mind and put her back on track. She had a light breakfast and then got dressed for town.

Viv came out to meet her at reception and ushered her in to her office. Lizzie was aware that Viv was chatting and friendly but could only hear her voice as though from a distance. Sitting down, she looked at Viv and was shocked to find herself crying.

'Viv, I killed her and I'm not sorry. I should be free and happy now, but I'm not. She has phoned me again, so I know she is still here. How can that be when I killed her?'

Viv swallowed and said, 'Lizzie, you are distraught, and I think that the alcohol and medicine together, have produced these symptoms. You must consider going to the Abbey clinic for a while. Henry is very worried and thinks along these lines too. We all want what is best for you.'

Lizzie wrung her hands and pleaded with Viv. 'Is there nothing stronger that you can give me? I promise I will not touch alcohol again, if you can just help me to avoid going there, to that place. I am so afraid that I will never come out again.'

Viv smiled at the wild-eyed woman and said gently, 'Lizzie, you are going to get through this, and in six months' time, we will joke about it.'

Lizzie shook her head sadly and said she doubted that she could be healed.

'Lizzie, I have seen so many women go for treatment and come out healed people. It's a wonderful place, a sanctuary, if you like, so peaceful and beautiful there, Henry and the children will be able to visit, you know. You will not be in solitary confinement or anything like that. I'll visit you and your friends can visit too. Now I am going to make a call to Professor Morgan and have a chat. He is the head of the Abbey clinic and a friend. He has a fantastic reputation and will sort you out.'

Viv rose and went around her desk and put her arms around Lizzie. 'I will just go, get his telephone number and talk to him. I'll be back in a minute.'

As she left the room, Lizzie dried her eyes and sighed. All she needed were a few strong pills. Her first medication had worked fine, after Marianne was born. Why had the medication after Mark not worked? She rested her elbows on the desk in front of her and put her head on her arms. After a few minutes she straightened up and noticed the pills on Viv's desk. She picked one of the containers up and looked at the label. Some sort of sedative, she thought; they looked like her first pills though. Looking over at the door, she guiltily slipped the pills into her handbag. If she was going to give up the alcohol, she would need all the sedation she could get!

Viv breezed back into the room, smiling. 'Well, that's sorted, Lizzie. Prof Morgan will see you first thing tomorrow at the clinic. If you want, I will accompany you, though I dare say, that Henry will insist upon going with you. He knows Morgan well. Now don't be worried Lizzie, try to relax and be positive about this.'

'What about the murder, Viv?' Lizzie asked quietly. 'Now I'm not even sure whether I did it or not.'

Viv stood before Lizzie and said, 'Lizzie, I don't think that you would have been capable of murdering her. You are so slight, and she was bigger than you and strong, I would say.'

Lizzie stood up and wrung her hands.

'I just don't know, now that she's phoned again. But I'm sure I can remember tying Henry's school tie around her neck.'

Viv looked appalled. 'You just heard reports on the news, Lizzie and imagined it. Why on earth would you do such a thing?'

'Because it was all his fault, having an affair with such a wicked person, and denying it all the time. He made me sick like this, it's all his fault.'

Lizzie spent the morning walking around the town aimlessly. She went to the park and sat on a bench looking at the ducks on the pond. What had happened to the perfect life that she now only vaguely remembered. She had walked Marianne and Mark all over this park, hadn't she? Where were her babies gone? Surely, they could not be the children who now lived in her house. How did they grow so quickly, where did those years go? She remembered the pills she had stolen and took them out. She needed calming now. She opened the container and took two out. She swallowed one and after a few minutes the other one. After an hour she felt more like walking again and got up. She went into a café and had a cup of coffee and felt much better, much calmer. As she got up to leave, she saw her friends Jenny and Sarah coming in. She smiled at them and they greeted her warmly. They asked how she was keeping as they had not seen her for ages, and she sat down with them and explained that she had not been so well. They sympathised with her and hoped that things would improve. Lizzie got such strength just then and calmly explained that she would probably have to go away for a while for treatment and that she hoped they would not forget her and visit her. They were quite amazed at this disclosure and assured her that they would always be there for her and they would mind her children while she was away. Lizzie nodded and smiled at them. The mist suddenly lifted from her head and she looked with love on these friends that she trusted. Suddenly, she felt energised and could not remember feeling so well in ages. They hugged each other warmly as they parted company and wished her all the best.

    Lizzie walked slowly home and wondered how it was that she felt so good. She thought it must be the pills she had taken and was relieved and happy. She thought she would have no need of alcohol if she continued to feel like this. The great feeling only lasted a couple of hours though, and the dark thoughts and fears descended, worse than ever, in the afternoon. It was unbearable, it was more horrifying than before. She rushed to her bedroom and feverishly searched for a bottle of vodka. She knew there was one somewhere, but where? At last she found it, in her locker. She gulped some down, her hands shaking so much that she spilt some down her front. She lay down on her bed and tried to relax. The children would be home soon, and she could not remember which activities were scheduled for today. She hoped she would not need to take the car out anywhere.

When later, she awoke, she went downstairs and took two more of the pills with a cup of coffee. Unable to stay still, she decided to go out again and walk. She thought she should buy a bottle of vodka, just in case she needed it. She told Ivy she would not be long.

    She walked all around the park, stopping at the north entrance and looking over at Linda's house. She stared at the building and imagined herself going up those steps. Did I really go up there, she wondered? Eventually she turned back and went to the off-licence and bought a bottle of vodka.

Henry spoke with Viv and then rang Professor Morgan. He gave him Lizzie's history and mentioned also her mother's suicide. He wondered how long the treatment might take. He spoke for about an hour with the man and felt only slightly reassured. It seemed to Henry that Lizzie had crossed some line and was a little beyond the normal borders. He blamed himself for that. He would have liked to have been able to blame Grace for not divulging her mother's illness earlier, or Viv, for not seeing that treatment was needed before this. In all honesty though, he could only blame himself for being too busy to see what was happening in front of him. What sort of a husband had he been and what sort of a father? He thought of his own dear father and felt ashamed. That man had never stinted his time with his son, was always aware of his achievements and full of encouragement and praise. When had *he* been half aware of his children's activities or achievements? When had he last praised them? If all this passed and Lizzie was cured, he vowed that his life would be different. He would never again be found wanting and he so wanted to feel proud of himself, both as a husband and a father.

Chapter 14

Marianne was playing her new piece of music and was really enjoying it. Her teacher was very surprised with her progress and asked her if she would like to consider doing a piano examination. Marianne, always cautious, asked her what exactly that would mean. The piano teacher explained all about what was required and told her that she only put pupils in for exams, who she knew would pass easily and Marianne was one of them. So, Marianne was full of fire and enthusiasm and thought it was a great idea and something of a challenge too. Some of her friends also did music with the same teacher.

She did not see her mother on returning home and understood that she was out. Ivy was busy making shepherd's pie in the kitchen, which she knew the children loved. Mark threw his bag down in the hall and immediately went out again. He was going to his friend across the road, which he often did. He knew that so long as he was in for dinner and before his father arrived, he was safe enough. Ivy would never tell tales.

Lizzie came home around five o'clock and Ivy thought that she looked very shook. She made her a cup of tea and asked if she was alright. Lizzie shook her head and told her that her doctor wanted her to go away for special treatment. She cried then, and

Ivy wrapped her arms around the overly thin woman and comforted her. She pleaded with her not to worry, she would take care of the children and that maybe this was for the best. She would come home soon, cured. But Lizzie shook her head and confessed that she did not think that she could be cured.

'There is something in me that is broken, Ivy. I just know it. I don't think it can be fixed you know?'

Ivy felt desperately sad for the poor woman.

'Of course, they will fix it all up, that is exactly how my daughter felt.'

She tried to think of something she could offer Lizzie that would put things in a positive light. 'Think about your children; you will be able to see them grow up and be proud of them and they, of you. Surely it's worth this little bit of inconvenience to get better?'

Lizzie nodded slowly. 'Thank you, Ivy, it will be bearable I suppose. I must do it for the children. I owe it to them.' She turned to Ivy and said, 'You are the best thing to have happened to me, and to my family. I could not cope without you, Ivy. For the sake of my children I will try my best, I promise, and I know you will be my main support, Ivy,'

'That's the way to think my dear, all will be well, you'll see. You must stay positive and I'll always be here for you, my dear.'

Later, as the children were eating dinner, Henry arrived. They were surprised to see him so early. Marianne told him about the piano exam that she was going to do and looked at him expectantly. He was so preoccupied that he did not reply, and the child looked away, disappointed. Mark looked at his sister and rolled his eyes.

Lizzie was in the sitting room. She was not very hungry she had said to the children. Mark immediately said, 'Can we have your share then?'

Lizzie told them to eat it all up. When the children had gone upstairs to finish their homework and prepare for bed, Henry went in and sat beside Lizzie. He tried to take her hand, but she pulled it away from him and moved further down the sofa.

'We must talk, Lizzie,' he said.

She turned to him and said, 'Yes, I suppose you know all about my being put away? Aren't you delighted? I'm not sorry you know, for killing that woman, don't think I am.'

Henry tried to talk reasonably to her and explained the different treatments available. The fact that the Abbey Centre was so close was a bonus, he said. Lots of visitors, and the children won't feel that you are far away. He tried to make it sound like an adventure and a very short one.

'Look Lizzie, I will contact Grace and maybe she could come and stay for a while, so you won't be worried about the children.'

He looked at his wife, but she made no comment. Neither did she look at him.

He sighed dejectedly and said, 'I do not for a moment believe that you killed Linda, you are not capable of that.'

Lizzie just said, 'I'm going to bed.'

She glanced into her daughter's room when passing by and smiled when she saw her at the piano. Going over, she touched Marianne on the arm and the child stopped playing and removed her headphones.

'Play for me Marianne,' she asked. The girl looked pleased and started to play her best piece, she was really very good and played with great expression, surprising Lizzie. When she was finished, she looked at her mother.

Lizzie looked at her puzzled, 'Where did you get that talent from, I wonder? Nobody in the family has that gift.'

Marianne was delighted and very glad that her mother liked her playing.

'What was the name of that piece Marianne?'

The little girl said, 'The name of the piece is Traumerai, which means, 'Daydreaming' and it's by Robert Schumann.'

Lizzie smiled and said, 'It's beautiful.'

She then said goodnight. Mark was in bed reading and Lizzie went over and kissed him goodnight. He smiled up at her. 'You missed the best shepherd's pie, ever,' he grinned.

She smiled and said, 'Next time I won't, you scamp.'

Alone, Lizzie thought about Grace. It would be wonderful if she could come down for a week or two. She sat on the bed and reached into her locker for the bottle of vodka. Her mind wandered to the meeting with Viv. Could they fix her? She remembered the tablets that she had stolen and felt guilty. Taking her bag, she looked at the bottle and wondered if they were the same as she had taken before. They seem to work, she thought. I have only had four so far, and they did help. She had walked the streets of the town today, her insides churning and her body desperately craving the ease and relaxation the medication brought, even if it was only temporary. She opened the bottle and took two more tablets out, her usual amount. She took them with the vodka and then sat on her chair by the window waiting for them to work. What would Grace think of her when she told her of the murder? Will the police finally realise that it was me? What will they do then? She had never given any thought to the outcome of the murder. Nobody believes me anyway, she thought. Not Viv, not Henry. Do I believe it? Did I just want to do it, as Viv suggests?

When she woke up it was dark outside, and her feet felt numb. Her mouth was so dry, and she had trouble moving her tongue. I must go to bed, she thought. She had trouble undressing, especially undoing her buttons. She fumbled her way to bed and had trouble getting under the duvet. I must have drunk too much she thought. Her mind continued it's tortuous, never ending circles.

Later she awoke and there was someone in her room. She tried to turn her head around to see who it was. Her head wouldn't move. Then out of the corner of her eye, she saw her. A woman, all dressed in white. Holding out her arms to her and smiling. Lizzie knew that face from somewhere far, far away. She did not feel at all frightened. She lay looking sideways at the lady and felt that she knew her, but where had she met her? The lady beckoned her to come to her still smiling. Lizzie tried to move her legs and tried to turn back the duvet, but her limbs were so heavy, so heavy, it was impossible. She could not move a muscle. The room was swimming in a soft golden light and still the lady stayed where she was, arms outstretched. Lizzie made a superhuman effort and felt herself floating out of her bed. Yes, she was floating away, her arms outstretched too, going towards the figure that she now recognised as her mother.

Next morning Henry had breakfast with the children and Ivy had arrived, happy and smiling as always. He decided he would go up and tell Marianne that Grace was coming that day and that he would come back at twelve to accompany her to see Dr. Morgan.

He stood at the door of her room and gave her the news. She was looking towards him, her eyes open. She did not make any comment, and he asked, 'Well, aren't you glad that Grace is coming to stay awhile?'

He was almost going to turn around and go back downstairs, exasperated as usual by her lack of response to him. Something made him pause and he moved further into the room and looked down at Lizzie. He saw that she was not breathing. His wife was dead, a most peaceful look on her face. All he could do was look down at her and shake his head. Tears ran down his face and he didn't realise that he was shouting 'No, no,' until Ivy appeared by his side and silently took in the situation and led him downstairs to his children.

When Marianne and Mark saw their father's face, they immediately knew that their mother was dead and started crying, but in a controlled way. Ivy left them together in the kitchen as the three stood with their arms around each other.

Chapter 15

All the community rallied around the bereft family. Lizzie's elderly father and all her family attended the funeral. Grace and her family stayed for two weeks, then, after John and her children had left, Grace stayed on. The neighbours were all wonderful and Henry did not know how he would have managed without their support. His colleagues were all very understanding and accommodating.

It was understood that Lizzie had overdosed on her medication. Henry did not want to believe it was suicide, but he just did not know. She had been so confused of late and imagined all sorts of things. The alcohol did not help of course. There would be no postmortem or inquest as she had seen her doctor the day before and Viv was able to give documentation to the effect that her patient had been under great stress and was due to go into treatment. She would say that her patient probably took too many tablets in error or forgetfulness.

The children were sad but very self-contained. They knew only too well how erratic their mother had been, for as long as they could remember. Marianne told her father and Grace about the voices and sounds that her mother often heard. They got on with their lives very quickly and seemed to have accepted her death well. Henry was a different matter. He was seized with feelings of guilt at not having had Lizzie sent away for professional treatment sooner. Grace, Henry and Viv met a few times at the house. Grace believed that her sister had suffered the same psychiatric illness as their mother but of course did not want to consider suicide. Viv agreed with Grace and told Henry that she should have insisted earlier that she go away for treatment.

Grace and Viv got on very well together. The more Grace told Viv the more Viv understood how it was with Lizzie. She had called by that day to ask Grace if she needed help to clear out Lizzie's clothes. She had to do it when her mother died, and it had been an awful ordeal. Grace was touched at Viv's thoughtfulness. She asked Viv if she would have any use for Lizzie's medicines and would she go through them as she would know what to discard if they were of no use? She had already sorted all Lizzie's clothes out and had them in boxes in the garage. She asked Viv if she would take a couple of boxes to the charity shops and she would take the rest. That way, they would all be gone the next day. Grace did not want to have Henry looking at them. She would soon have to return home to her own family. Viv told Grace that she would keep an eye on the family and Henry. She did not work as many hours as he did, and Viv said she could bring the kids to activities when they and she were free. Grace was very appreciative. They agreed to keep in touch with each other.

The inquest on Linda Smythe concluded that the woman had been attacked in her home and stabbed to death in the hours following her last sighting at the gym, as she was still in her gym clothing. A time could not be decided on. The police were investigating the significance of a school tie, which had been put on the dead woman, after death, apparently. They were investigating that at present. The only fingerprints that were found, were on the hall door, and it seemed likely that they belonged to a female, being quite small.

A new man was now professor of psychiatry at the university and was a very different person to Smythe, everybody agreed. He had different ideas and was very modern in his approach. He also did not like the idea of amalgamation and did not agree that big, so-called 'centres of excellence', were always better.

Henry brought the children to visit his mother as often as possible and the longer holidays, he brought them up to the farm, where they felt most at home.

Winter saw them all more-or-less, settled into normal life. Ivy continued to come and housekeep and cook for them. Henry cut down on his private clinics but had still had two evenings to work. He made a point of being home by six o'clock most evenings from the hospital and if he was late, Ivy would stay on, until he arrived.

His communication with the children improved a lot. Poor Lizzie had made it very difficult to have a normal home life, with her suspicions of him, which was really paranoia. He felt younger than he had in years.

His mother and Betts came down now and again and they were planning to celebrate Christmas this year with Henry in his house, for a change. The children were looking forward to it. Henry was dreading it, remembering last Christmas and how strained it was. He need not have worried. Ivy prepared lots of Christmas fare. The neighbours, Jenny and Kate came around with presents for the children and they were all invited to their houses for supper when Christmas Day was over. Henry was worried about whether it was too soon after Lizzie's death, but Jenny said that he must consider the children and that Lizzie would want them to enjoy the festivities. He knew in his heart they were right.

On Christmas Eve, there was a candlelit carol service at the school and the children were very excited. All their friends would be going and their parents and now Granny and Betts would be there too. All the children had a different part to play and it was a well organised affair and had been, for years.

Christmas Day passed off very well. They met all the neighbours and friends at church that morning and Henry bumped into Viv as they had the usual cup of tea and mince pies afterwards. He was surprised to see Viv there. 'Oh yes, I do occasionally come to church,' she said, on seeing his surprise. 'I just love Christmas, I always have.'

'What do you do for Christmas dinner, Viv? Do you cook yourself a turkey or what?' Henry was concerned at the thought of Viv eating all alone. He did not know anything about her family.

Viv replied, 'I will do what I always do, travel to my elderly uncle, who is in a home. I have dinner with him, although I'm not sure if he knows who I am any more,' she laughed. 'I like being there with him, even if he does confuse me sometimes with his sister. There are so many old folks there with nobody to sit and eat dinner with them. Then we all sit around the Christmas tree and a local group comes in with various musical instruments, and we sing carols. It is all rather lovely.'

Henry thought that it was very noble of Viv, but as she explained, he was all the family she had, and she also had a duty to visit him as often as possible. He invited her to come and visit then before the New Year for a drink and meet his mother and sister. She promised she would.

The children had set the table beautifully and Henry was very proud of them. His mother oversaw everything and made sure all that was needed was provided. She and Betts had done last minute shopping on Christmas Eve morning and there was enough food and drink to see them into the New Year.

Betts cooked the dinner which was excellent. Henry wondered why he ever worried about his young sister. She could cater for anyone. His mother was in good spirits and was interested in life again. Compared to last year, this Christmas was cosy and warm and everyone enjoyed themselves. They played charades after dinner and Betts excelled at that. Then they all settled down to a movie before going to bed by eleven, tired out but very content.

The holiday period continued lazily, with walks in the morning to the park, the children with their skateboards or bicycles. Betts was delighted to see so much of her niece and nephew and their grandmother so protective and proud of her only son.

They had supper one night with Jenny and her lovely family and another night with Kate. Viv called by the evening before New Year's Eve, and they sat and had a drink with Henry's mother Iris, and Betts. New Year's Eve and Day were celebrated quietly, and the children were happy to play with their new electronic games and devices. Then it was all over, and time for school to start again and Henry to resume his work at the hospital. He knew it would be strange getting back to normal again after the holiday period. He was not prepared for the emptiness though. He threw himself into his work and research and looked forward to extending the services in his department. He had a great team working with him and they all enjoyed their work. It was demanding of course, but all aspects of medicine are, and he reasoned that no one would go into medicine unless they were fully committed.

It was at the hospital during a meeting with other junior doctors and psychiatric students and nurses that he had a visit from the local police one Saturday morning. While they were having a coffee break, he was chatting to Viv. The pharmaceutical industry was singling out various clinics like theirs and were really trying to push their newest products. Henry thought they all needed to be prepared for this and urged caution and restraint until the drugs were satisfactorily researched. Viv touched his arm and nodded in the direction of the approaching policemen.

They apologised for coming to the hospital but explained it had been difficult to find him and they would like to have a chat with him, at home, if that was possible. Henry was surprised and wondered what they could possibly want to talk to him about. He suggested they come to the house that afternoon when the meeting had finished, and he would be happy to speak with them. When they had left, he turned to Viv and wondered what that was all about? She thought that it might concern Lizzie and that she could come around that afternoon and be there too. He agreed but was puzzled about why it was necessary for the police to want to talk to him at all. When he went home after lunch, he rang Jenny and asked if the children could possibly come to her that afternoon as he was expecting a visit from the police. She agreed of course and wondered if everything was alright and if there was anything else that she could do. Henry told her it was a casual visit he expected and might be about Lizzie's death. He promised to keep her informed.

At three thirty, Viv arrived at the house and they both sat drinking coffee waiting for the police to come by. Henry asked Viv what she felt about the visit. Viv hesitated and then put down her cup of coffee. She said, 'Henry, there is something that you should know. When Lizzie visited my clinic, the day that I last saw her, well, sometime later, maybe days later, I discovered that a bottle of pills was missing from my desk. I know that I should not have had them there, but I was reading up the information on them. There were several bottles of different sedatives and anti-psychotic drugs. They were a new batch of drugs, samples that the pharmaceutical company send out every so often. It was only after Liz's death that I connected the two things and I wondered whether Liz had taken them, as she had requested some medication that day. Seeing as how she was going to see Dr. Morgan the next day, I declined to prescribe anything else. Now I feel bad about it all. I am assuming that it was Liz who took them. In any case, I am guilty of negligence.'

Henry shook his head. 'Viv, that is something that we shall never know. If she did take any, she would not have thought it might kill her, would she? It doesn't mean that she committed suicide, does it?'

Viv shook her head. 'Henry, I do not for a moment think that she did. She never knew how her mother died and she did so want to get better. The doorbell rang, it was four o'clock.

Chapter 16

The two men on the doorstep were not in uniform They identified themselves and Henry invited them inside. It soon turned out that they were not inquiring about Lizzie's death. They were making inquiries about Professor Smythe and had some questions for Henry. They were surprised to see another person present and asked who she was and why she was present. Henry explained that Viv was a family friend and had been his wife's doctor.

The questions turned to Linda's murder and Henry explained where he was on the Tuesday she was last seen. He explained about getting a phone call from his mother and leaving straight away to rush to the hospital to see his father. He told them the time he reached the hospital and of his father's death. The men expressed sympathy. One of them then produced a tie in a plastic bag and asked him if he recognised the tie. Henry peered at the tie and said he recognised it as a school tie. 'It's a school tie, St. Albans's, where I once was a pupil, many years ago.'

'And do you have such a tie, sir?' the older man asked.

'Well, I'm sure I have one, somewhere, but I have not seen it in years. I stopped going to reunions years ago, mainly because all my past friends have moved on or emigrated. Besides, it's rather a long way to travel for an evening out.'

The younger man coughed and asked if it was possible that he had it here in the house. Henry looked puzzled and said he did not know, but could they wait, and he would go up to his room and look in his wardrobe?

They looked at one another and the older man said, 'That would be very helpful, sir.'

Henry left the room. Viv turned to the detectives and asked if they would like tea or coffee? They both declined. She then reminded them that Henry's wife had recently died and that he was still grieving. They asked her about her relationship with his wife. What exactly was she being treated for? She explained that she specialised in women's mental health and worked at the nearby maternity hospital. They nodded and one wrote in his notebook.

'So, she was being treated for psychiatric problems, was she?'

Viv was annoyed and let them know it. 'You must know that a doctor cannot divulge information about a patient. You may ask her husband I suppose.'

She got up and went to the kitchen with her and Henry's used coffee cups. She heard Henry re-enter the room and joined them.

Henry shrugged at the men and confessed that he could not find the tie, if it had been there at all, he could not remember when he had last seen it.

Viv said, 'Henry, is it not possible that it was left at home, in your mother's house? Have you any stuff left there can you remember?'

Henry spread his hands. 'It may be there, on the other hand, my Mum could have chucked all my old stuff out or more likely, given it to the charity shops. Why are you so keen to find out if it belongs to me?'

The older man told them that it had been found around the dead woman's neck. Henry looked shocked. 'But I thought that she was stabbed to death, that's what it said in the papers.' He looked from Viv to the men.

The younger man explained that the tie was not the cause of death and had seemingly been placed around the dead woman's neck, shortly after she had been killed.

'Very shortly, we think, possibly immediately after she was dead.'

They rose to their feet and apologised for upsetting him and asked if he wouldn't mind contacting his mother to try and locate his tie. Viv then asked them if they had found anyone else in the town or surrounding areas that might have also attended this school.

'Henry surely, was not the only pupil in that school,' she said sarcastically. Have you done a bit of research into the matter?'

The two men turned to look at her and the older man said, 'Madam, we do quite thorough research, and Dr. Dukes is the only one in this area or county who attended St. Alban's.'

They took their leave and left Henry feeling lost and shocked. He kept remembering Lizzie's dreams of blood and her confession to having killed Linda. He sat on the sofa in silence and gazed into the distance. Viv sat down beside him.

'Oh God, Viv, could poor Lizzie have killed Linda, do you think? She told me that she did, but I didn't believe her, I mean, how could she have done it, she would not have had the strength, and why the tie? She was stabbed not strangled.'

Viv patted his hand. 'Henry, I would say the same as you, but for something that Liz told me, at one session. She mentioned putting a tie around Linda's neck and said that it was your tie.'

Henry looked in horror at Viv. 'I also did not believe her. I asked her why your tie and she said that she wanted you to be blamed for the murder.'

Henry put his head in his hands and rocked to and fro.

Viv continued, 'When they produced the tie, I immediately remembered something being said about a tie. As far as we know, it could be one of Lizzie's delusions or fantasies. It still might not be your tie, anyone could pick a tie up at a charity shop, couldn't they?'

Henry, shook his head and asked Viv what he should do? 'If Mum cannot find my old tie, what does it look like? Poor Lizzie, I can't believe that she would have been capable.'

Viv said soothingly, 'If it is your tie, there will surely be DNA or something to connect you. If it is your tie, you had nothing to do with where it was placed. You were on your way north that Tuesday, if it was that day she was murdered, and you were away for more than a week. I would say there is no evidence to connect you to Linda's death. Lizzie was with you up there for the funeral so from where I am sitting, it seems the police have nothing on either of you.'

Henry would not be placated. 'Isn't it strange that she should tell you about the tie business, Viv? She could not have just made something like that up. There has to be more to it than that.'

Viv thought for a while. 'Well the only other explanation is that she did kill her, as unlikely as it seems.'

Henry turned to Viv, ashen faced. 'Should I go and explain to the police about her rantings and ravings, Viv?'

'What will it sound like, Henry? A man whose school tie is missing, who has known history with that awful woman and is now blaming his dead wife?' She shook her head, her lip trembling and tears running down her face. 'I don't think you can say anything Henry, without implicating yourself, no matter how good your alibi is.'

She started sobbing and Henry did not know what to do. He felt like crying himself. How did he ever get into a mess like this? He who was always so successful at everything he did. It all started with that awful woman and he felt that if she was still alive, he would now go out and kill her with his bare hands.

He put his arms around Viv and comforted her and said, 'I will listen to you Viv, I am a complete disaster area. Come on, we need a drink before the kids come back.'

He rang his mother that night and enquired about the tie. He felt greatly relieved when his mother confessed to having put all his old school clothing into the local charity shop. The next day he called into the police station before going to work and left a note for the two detectives telling them the news and leaving his mother's telephone number with them, in case they needed to confirm it with her themselves.

The children continued to thrive, and Henry felt that they were taking advantage of him regularly. He was too preoccupied to care very much. What preyed on his mind most was the fact that Lizzie hated him so much that she wanted him blamed for Linda's murder. Was he that bad? What sort of conception of him had she, in her poor twisted mind? She obviously never believed him, that he was not having an affair with Linda. What about the telephone calls she complained about? Were they real? He then remembered about the night that he went to the jazz club and Lizzie had complained the next night, when he rang her at her family home, of hearing music in the background. He pondered on this, remembering his frustration with her and annoyance. He knew that he did not ring her at the jazz club. He had left his phone there behind him. Suppose someone had rung from his phone? That was rubbish, he told himself. It may have happened that someone sat on the phone and it just hit the number of her phone. He could no longer remember whether she said the caller left a message. He needed a chat with Grace. She could help him think straight.

Chapter 17

The children were delighted at the idea of going up to the farm and seeing their cousins. It was still cold, and they hoped there might be snow. Marianne had fantasies of being snowed in and unable to move back home for months. Mark worried a bit about missing his football match that weekend and was afraid that he might be dropped from the team. His Dad reassured him that it was just a once-off and that he had called the coach and explained.

Grace was happy to see them all. She knew by looking at Henry that he was not alright. She bided her time and when all the social talking was over, she brought him to the local pub, and they sat in a quiet place to chat. She listened patiently to the episode of the police visit and the conversation between himself and Viv afterwards.

She could not for a moment think that her sister would be capable of killing anyone. She was a slight woman, not strong enough to wield a knife surely. But even she, could not think of any logical reason for the tie being left on the dead woman. She could accept suicide however, as she told Henry, seeing as their mother was driven to it by her illness. Her advice to Henry finally was, when they had exhausted themselves debating the issue, to put everything out of his mind. Let the police do their work, throw himself into *his* work and if things developed, well so be it. How could poor Lizzie be charged with anything now?

It did not snow, and Henry returned home on Sunday evening, a little more relaxed than he had been. Grace was right of course. How could a dead woman be charged with murder, whether she did it or not? He just did not want to think of Lizzie as a murderer.

He threw himself into work as Grace advised and at the end of that week felt much more invigorated and alive.

The next week the hospital was buzzing with gossip. A newly qualified doctor, Luke Pattison, had been brought into the police station to be questioned about his relationship with Linda Smythe. Obviously rumours had been repeated to the police, when they first interviewed the professional colleagues of the professor. Furthermore, it appeared that he was also a past pupil of St. Alban's. He was asked to produce his tie and was, like Henry, having trouble locating it. When Henry heard about this, he felt so sorry for the doctor involved. The police were certain that the murderer was someone whom the professor knew and was likely to be someone in the medical field and possibly a colleague. Luke's mother met with Viv and the poor woman was beside herself with worry and grief. She had no idea of his relationship with Linda and was also mortified at the idea of her son and a much older woman. Viv reassured her that it would probably blow over and she also gave the woman an insight into the character of Linda. The mother contacted some of his best friends and asked for their help. They had of course, known about Luke's predicament.

Somebody had a bright idea and put a page up on Facebook, explaining about Luke's unwanted involvement with his boss and asking if there were any more people out there who had been in the same position. The response was immediate and considerable. The number of doctors who claimed to have been the target of Professor Smythe's attention greatly outnumbered any other female doctors. Not only that, some were historical cases going back about twenty years.

Henry was not a social media person, so he knew nothing about the furore, until another doctor mentioned it in the hospital. Henry could hardly believe it. In his naivety, he thought that he was unique, the only one singled out for her attention. He now felt sorry that he had never mentioned his problem to others when it happened. Maybe it would have warned or prepared other young doctors of what she was after. He felt for the young doctor and suddenly decided to go and tell the police of his experience too.

Detective Jones was surprised to see Henry and thanked him for coming in. Henry explained that he had to let them know the sort of woman Linda was, and felt that it was his duty to do it. The detective smiled and said that female harassment happened in all professions but was never really made public. For men who depended on their female employers for references or advancement, it was the same sticky situation for them, just as the same situation pertained to women. Henry felt pleased with himself and got up to return to work. Jones told him that they were aware of the response to Luke's friends' Facebook page. They explained that they would get in touch with anyone they thought might be a suspect in the case, but explained it was a local crime and it was committed by someone in the vicinity, who knew the professor's movements. It did not help that Luke Pattison was also a member of the same gym as Linda Smythe. However, later that day, Luke was given the all clear and was free to carry on with his life. He was not told why he was no longer a suspect and all his colleagues felt great relief.

Henry and the children had supper regularly with Jenny and family or Kate and they were already familiar with the rumours and gossip which went back and forwards across the town. Henry never told anyone of course, about Lizzie's claims to have murdered the professor. It was nobody's business except his.

Viv was not pleased that Henry had gone to the police. She felt that it put him in danger himself. She felt the less he seemed to be involved, the better. Let the police do their work. He admitted that it had been a spur of the moment decision to show solidarity with Luke Pattison. Many other young doctors were doing the same and the police even heard from doctors outside the country who had experienced Smythe's attention. Henry told Viv that the police now realised that there might be a lot of people out there that had reason to murder Linda. Viv agreed and said that it was time to get on with his life. He smiled wryly at that and asked, 'I feel as though my life is mostly over, there has been too much trauma in it, Viv'.

She smiled and hugged him and told him that he had not lived a proper life for a long time.

'So, relax, get out and enjoy life, Henry. There is a great big world out there. You are a well-qualified professional and you deserve the best that life can offer.'

He looked at her and smiled, shaking his head.

'I don't think I understand the meaning of the word anymore. I must keep going of course for the children. They deserve so much, and I am not sure that I can deliver anything. I'm just an empty shell.'

Viv assured him that he was a wonderful father and that they were children he could be proud of.

'What about the Annual Hospital Dinner Dance, next week? Are you thinking of attending?'

Henry admitted that he had never attended the event, since Lizzie got sick.

'Well Dr. Dukes, will you do me the honour of accompanying me to the same event?'

Henry looked at Viv. 'I am not sure that I will be great company, Viv, but if you are asking me to go, then why not? You will have to excuse any social awkwardness from me, I haven't been at one of these things for years.'

Viv was delighted and squeezed his arm. 'There you are, we'll get you back into the swing of things, you'll see.'

Later, Henry regretted having committed to going. The idea of dressing up in an evening suit made him feel ill. He told the children that he was going to a special adult party and they were enthralled at the idea. He told Ivy and she was happy and asked him to take out what he would be wearing and that she would make sure it was dry cleaned if necessary, and his shirt pressed. She thought he might need a new pair of shoes. She had noticed that he only had a brown pair and an ordinary black pair. She suggested that he should go into the city and get a decent pair of dress shoes. He listened to the motherly woman and was thankful again, that he had found such a wonderful creature. Sometimes he felt guilty about how little attention he paid to Ivy. Lizzie had mentioned at some stage of her illness that Ivy was the only person who understood her, having a daughter who had also suffered from postnatal depression. He decided that in future, he must show Ivy more consideration and attention. She was so vital for their welfare and it was only right that he should show it.

When he found the right pair of shoes, he proudly showed them to Ivy. 'Well, what do you think, Ivy, are they up to the job?'

Ivy considered them and chuckled. 'They are gorgeous, doctor, and I just hope they are as comfortable as they look, you will have to dance, you know.'

Henry laughed. 'I have not danced in years and I hope Viv won't be expecting a Fred Astaire or she will be sorely disappointed. Tell me Ivy, do you not think it may be considered bad taste by attending this thing, I mean, so soon after Lizzie?'

Ivy put down the iron she was using and said very seriously, 'Doctor, your good late wife was not a well lady for some time. If she is where I hope she is, and where we all hope to go when we die, I would bet that she is urging you to go and enjoy yourself.'

Enjoy it he did, despite his qualms. He had a lot of colleagues coming up and shaking his hand and saying how thrilled they were to see him out. He had never realised how isolated his life had been. Viv introduced him to some of her friends whom he had never met. The dinner was excellent, and the company was exhilarating for Henry. He now appreciated how starved he had been of human friendship and camaraderie. He felt very relaxed. Dancing was not so good though. He was very much out of touch there. Poor Viv did not complain although her feet surely would be sore tomorrow, he thought.

There was a slight awkwardness on the return journey. When he dropped Viv home, she had asked if he would like to come in for a nightcap. Henry immediately felt uncomfortable and declined. He was worried that the children might be awake and waiting for him, as it was unusual for them to have a babysitter, he explained. He knew it sounded lame, but he knew he did not want to be alone with Viv, although it would have been impossible for him to say why, he did not understand it himself. Viv understood and let it pass.

'Henry, you must just be yourself and don't feel any pressure at all. Understand? You have a lot of friends, you know. It might take you a while to get to the stage of knowing that you are free again, to live whatever sort of life you want.'

She patted his hand and thanked him for coming tonight. Henry got out of the driver seat and went around to open the door for her. He felt like an awkward teenager. He walked her to her door and thanked her for asking him to go. He had really enjoyed the company and the social aspect of the evening.

As Viv entered her house, she smiled at him and said, 'Now that you have broken the ice, we must find more entertainment for you. You are not made for a solitary existence.'

He laughed and turned to walk back to his car.

'I mean it, Henry! I'll be in touch,' she promised.

He waved back at her and got into his car.

After the babysitter had left, Henry sat in the sitting room with a whiskey and thought about the evening. He was not tired, although normally he would have been. He thought about the lonely and solitary lives that both he and Lizzie had led. He thought about all the holidays and outings that they should have had together, the fun that they should have had, the good memories they should have accumulated. Where were they? He sipped his drink and realised, there were no happy memories, not since Marianne had been born. He felt very sad.

Chapter 18

Marianne and Mark were growing rapidly, it seemed to their father. Mark grew out of his clothes so quickly and Marianne was getting so confident and chatty, it made Henry feel old.

His work was again building up into what it had been before Lizzie died. The clinics increased. He was also expected to tutor students, and he really wanted to devote more time to research and writing. The annual conference would be in Holland this year and he really was looking forward to that. He did not know if he would have a paper ready in time. He was more relaxed about it. He did not have to put forward a paper every year, let others do it.

He attended a few of his local family meetings. The ones that he had originally set up to provide support for parents of children with ADD or ADHD. He was getting to know these people as friends, not parents of patients and he enjoyed it. They were wonderful people he thought.

The meetings were not that regular, maybe once every six weeks. Viv had offered to babysit whenever he was stuck. Ivy was not always available to babysit as she had family commitments of her own.

On one such evening, Viv had stepped in at the last moment to mind the children. It was lucky she had, he felt afterwards.

On arriving, Viv asked where Marianne was. Mark told her she was sulking in her bedroom and rolled his eyes at her, as though to say 'Girls!'
Viv went up to Marianne's room and found the girl, pale and anxious.

'Whatever is wrong, Marianne? Are you alright? Viv was concerned at the pallor of the girl. Marianne looked at Viv and said, 'There is something wrong with me, Viv, I'm bleeding. I think I am going to die, like Mum.'

After inquiring about the bleeding, Viv laughed and said gently, 'Marianne, all females bleed like this, when they reach a certain age. Did you not know?'

Marianne looked shaken. 'But why, Viv?'

So it was, that Viv had to explain what happened to girls approaching their teens. She told Marianne that she had been fifteen when it happened. Marianne was rather young, only ten, but sometimes it happened like that. She reassured the young girl that she would not die and that all was normal. She told her that she would go to the local store now and get her what was necessary.

She was gone ten minutes and Marianne was sorted out and feeling more at ease. Mark had been observing the coming and going of Viv and the activity upstairs. He slipped up and was eavesdropping at the door in case he was missing something important, when he got the gist of what was happening to his sister. He was horrified and appalled. Then he was discovered crouched at the door when the ladies came out to go downstairs. His face told Viv that he had been listening.

'Are you alright Mark? Were you earwigging on ladies' conversation?'

'Is this going to happen to me too?' He gulped and looked scared and disgusted at the same time.

'Of course not, Mark. Boys and men are spared that suffering, lucky things.'

Viv laughed at him and so did Marianne. She was now a club member of something that he could never join. She smirked at him as she went down the stairs after Viv. Mark was very relieved and went down the stairs after them.

Henry was relieved that Viv was there for that drama and felt she did a better job than he would have done. He felt rather inadequate for that part of the children's development and Viv told him that he should start reading a few parenting books on these sensitive subjects. He promised that he would.

Marianne had a rather special bond with Viv after that and the two of them would spend a lot of time looking at fashion magazines and discussing girly affairs. Mark did not mind too much as he knew that Viv had a very soft spot for him, and he looked forward to their ice-skating time and Saturday movies. They often went back to Viv's house for supper or a barbeque at weekends, when Henry was on duty or busy and Ivy did not work at weekends.

During the week Henry received a telephone call from the local police station, requesting him to come in when it was convenient. Surprised and a little unquiet about it, he went in one morning and met the two detectives he had met previously. They explained that they would appreciate his agreeing to a DNA test to eliminate him from the tie found at the crime scene. They explained that Dr. Pattison had already been in and they were the only two in this town who had been to St. Alban's school. There would be more in other parts of the country no doubt. He felt reassured at this and agreed readily. It was over in minutes and he was ready to leave, when one of the detectives asked him to sign a form stating that he had not been coerced in any way. He thought that both detectives looked at each other after he signed the form. But they said 'Goodbye', pleasantly enough, as he left the room.

    He thought no more about it as Holland was on his mind. He wondered whether Grace would be free to come down and mind the children for the four days. Before he could contact her however, Viv asked about his plans and he confessed that he had not contacted Grace yet but was hopeful, as her children were older now and more self-sufficient. Viv then said that she would love to mind them, as they all got on so well, but suggested that Henry should consult them first.

The children happily agreed that they would like Viv to come and take care of them. They knew there would be treats and perhaps an ice-skating outing. Viv was easy to manipulate!

It was all arranged, Ivy would continue to come in and clean the house, they would cycle home with their next-door friends, do their homework while Ivy was there, eat their dinner and Viv would be at the house by six o'clock. If there was football, she would take Mark to that and Marianne to her piano lesson. Henry was delighted at how easily things were sorted out. He would now be able to go to Holland in a month's time with an easy mind and enjoy the conference. He had almost finished a paper too, he was quite happy about that, one on Autism and different aspects of it. He was so fulfilled in his work. It was the constant challenge of it all and the satisfaction in dealing with difficult cases. The research side of things had always appealed to him and he was forever devouring all the incoming medical magazines and learning about all the new drugs coming on the market. Keeping up with them all was the problem, it was all very time-consuming but necessary.

Chapter 19

A week before Henry was due to fly to Holland, he had another call from the police station requesting his presence, as soon as it was possible. He thought nothing of it as he drove in before work that morning. As soon as he saw both the detective's faces, he felt a moment of alarm. He was ushered into a side room which said 'Interview room 3' on the door.

Detectives Jones and Miller, immediately opened a file and looking at Henry, stated that his DNA had been found on the school tie. They looked at him as though waiting for an explanation. Of course, Henry had none and looked at them, shrugging his shoulders. They also said that they had noticed that he was left-handed. Again, Henry shrugged and asked what was so strange about that?

Jones explained that the professor had been stabbed by a left-handed person and that it must be obvious to him why they were interested in him. Miller said nothing but just stared at Henry, which Henry found very intimidating.

'I have already explained where I was that night; driving up to my mother as she was in the hospital with my dying father. How do you think I managed to kill her and be up there at the same time?'

Now Miller leaned forward, eagerly, it seemed to Henry, who tried desperately to follow the man's accent and explanation. There was no known date or time for the murder, it may have been that night or not. Who could tell when Linda was murdered? The weather was cold and there had been no heating on at her house; the body was well preserved. He leaned back and stared at Henry, in what Henry felt, was a hostile manner.

'But I was away for a week. Honestly this is ridiculous, I am being used as a scapegoat!'

The men smiled grimly and reminded Henry that as it was only two hour's drive away, it would have been very easy to leave any night and drive down and back, having murdered the woman.

Henry felt trapped and wondered whether he was dreaming. His brain refused to take in what the detectives were suggesting. By now, he was sweating profusely.

'What can I do to convince you that I have not murdered anyone? I am missing appointments in the hospital and must really leave now. I want to help all I can, but I am not the person who did this, honestly.'

'Dr. Dukes, you must get yourself a solicitor as soon as possible and return for a more formal interview. You must also surrender your passport, today, and it would be advisable to consult with your employer to arrange some leave of absence.'

There was no sign of sympathy or understanding on either face, even when he explained he was due to go to Holland in four days' time. He left the station feeling totally shattered and in a state of disbelief. This could not be happening to him, a consultant psychiatrist!

His boss and manager listened and agreed to arrange cover for him. He was totally sympathetic and did not for a moment believe what the police suspected. Henry left the office and drove home in a daze. He sat in the kitchen with Ivy and told her what was happening. Her advice was to get himself a good solicitor as soon as possible, which Henry agreed to do.

In the meantime, he put a call through to Viv and explained his situation. She was appalled and could only say, 'Oh Henry, Oh Henry!' He asked if she could stand in for him when he was at the station, as he had no idea at what time he would be back after the interview. Then he rang a friend of his, a solicitor whom he had known for years, and explained his situation to him. His friend said he would gladly represent him.

At the station they took his fingerprints and all his details, in the presence of his solicitor. As far as Henry could remember, they took all the same details again, asked all the same questions again and at the end of two hours, the man felt he had need of sedation.

By the end of the day, when the children and he were eating the dinner that Ivy had left them, he could not talk to, or answer the questions the children were plying him with. He just said he was very tired and upset and asked them to be patient with him. They retired to their bedrooms, subdued. They were aware of the rumours flying around the neighbourhood.

The next day the solicitor rang early in the morning, to say that he was compiling all the information in the event of a court case. He told Henry to take a couple of days off and go somewhere with the children for a bit of relaxation. He would deal with the police in the meantime.

Henry asked the children what they would like to do. They had a short discussion with each other and then said, Grace's cottage at the seaside. He rang Grace and checked with her. He had kept her informed of all the action taking place in his life. He knew he had a friend in Grace. He could tell her anything.

By lunchtime, there were at the seaside, eating fish and chips. Grace was coming later. It was not warm enough to swim but the children ran about, paddling and scrutinising the rock pools. Henry sat on a towel and watched them, wondering what had happened to change all their lives so suddenly.

Grace arrived later with a cooked casserole dinner and homemade bread and the children made quick work of it. When they were in bed Grace listened silently as Henry poured out all that had happened in the last week. She also could not believe that he was under suspicion. She asked him if he had told them of Lizzie's confession, her delusions and dreams of blood? Henry shook his head and stated that he was not about to make the police believe that Lizzie had committed murder.

'It's not Lizzie that is under suspicion, it's me, Grace.'

Grace understood but felt that it was not fair that the police only had half the story. She tried to reassure the broken man beside her, that the truth would come out, whatever it was and that he would be cleared of all suspicion of murder. Henry was not so confident.

On his return, he visited the solicitor and was surprised to find him so upbeat and optimistic about things. As far as he was concerned, there was no evidence at all except for the tie, which he felt could be there for any number of reasons. When they both arrived back at the station, the atmosphere was different, Henry felt. He was not sure in which way, it just was. There was still hostility, however. Now they were almost suggesting that two people were involved and wondered whether his fragile wife and himself had plotted to kill Smythe. As Henry looked at them askance, his solicitor intervened on his behalf.

Miller and Jones looked at each other and then pushed an open file across to the solicitor. The solicitor pushed if back and asked when this statement had been made.

Jones said, 'Doctor Mullen came in yesterday and voluntarily gave it. She felt that she had to put the record straight about Doctor Dukes' wife.'

'What about my wife?' asked Henry.

Miller said quietly to Henry, 'We understand now about your wife's illness doctor, you should have been more forthcoming, especially about her confession and the tie business.'

'My wife had nothing to do with the murder, I would swear to that. She was too slight in build for any sort of violence. I find her so-called, confession, impossible to believe. I think she was suffering from delusions at that point. Doctor Mullen told me that this is common.'

Jones interrupted, 'Doctor, you may be trying to protect your wife, but what Doctor Mullen revealed to us, shows a highly disturbed woman, very vulnerable but volatile perhaps.'

Henry shook his head and looked at his solicitor, who continued writing in his notebook.

'Then there is another angle, doctor,' said Miller. We think that two people were involved in this lady's murder, so we must consider if both you, and your wife, were involved. You could have motivated her, by your history, with Smythe.'

Henry could only shake his head sadly.

'My poor wife surely had motive to murder that woman, considering how she suffered from all the anonymous phone calls from her, that I, in my stupidity didn't believe.'

Miller and Jones looked down at the statement and then both looked up at Henry. The solicitor leaned over to Henry and shook his head.

'You don't have to say anything more, Henry. This is not the issue here.'

Henry said, 'Why can't I stand up for Lizzie. I know she was incapable of this crime and I certainly did not do it either.'

Miller said off-handedly, 'Tell us of the phone calls, if you would, doctor.'

Henry spent the next thirty minutes explaining about how the calls always came when he was not present and how upset Lizzie had been. No, he could not remember exactly when they began. She was on antidepressant medicine at that time, he was sure of that. He spoke of her growing paranoia, her meeting with Linda at the hotel and her certainty that it was Linda who was making the calls. He told them of Linda's seduction of him when a student, which he had already mentioned to them and how Lizzie, in her depressed state was convinced that he was still having an affair with the professor, which he assured the men, he was not.

'My biggest failure, as a husband, was my disbelief. It was only later, that I began to believe my wife.'

'Did you believe that it was the professor who was making the calls?' Miller asked.

'I think I did, otherwise who else?' Henry combed his fingers through his hair and stared at the ceiling.

The detective, Miller, closed the file then and stood up.

'That's it for today, gentlemen, you may go, and we will be in touch when we have more information. Thank you for your cooperation in all these matters.'

As the men got up to leave, Jones said that there was just one other matter. The fingerprints, found on the professor's hall door and sitting room door; they were not Henry's as they were too small, they were likely to be female. They wondered if Henry would be willing to let his children's DNA be taken for comparison? Henry was outraged and could not even reply. His solicitor whispered in his ear and Henry reluctantly agreed that they could do that.

Jones hoped that it was not too late for his trip to Holland. Henry said that he had no appetite now, to go anywhere. He just wanted his wife's name and his to be totally cleared.

One leaving the station, he turned to his solicitor and asked him, 'What now?'

Once again, the solicitor seemed upbeat and confident.

'If they had any evidence Henry, you would now be under arrest. They have not got a cat's whisker, so go and try not to worry about things.'

'What about Viv's statement, should she have done that, do you think? I'm not sure myself that it was a good thing. It could have put poor Lizzie more in the frame, don't you think?'

The solicitor did not offer his opinion and just told Henry to go and relax and when he, the solicitor heard anything more, he would be in touch with Henry. He had been very anxious in there a while back when Henry started talking off-the-cuff. He knew that although Viv wanted to show how psychotic Lizzie was, she could also have put Henry in the frame as well.

Next day, after arranging with Henry, a policewoman called to the house and took a sample of the children's DNA. They were very excited and wondered what it was all about. The woman was very friendly and explained that were doing a survey in different places to study scientific matters, to help in health surveys.

There was rare excitement at the same police station a week later. The fingerprints found in the basement flat of the professor's house were not Henry's but showed up on the data base; they were a match for some found at another murder scene, eighteen years previously in the south of the country. The two detectives involved in this case were jubilant! Could it be that they were going to solve two crimes at once, one an eighteen-year old cold case? Miller and Jones were dispatched very quickly to carry out investigations down at the seaside town. They knew that it would not be easy getting information dating eighteen years, but they knew patience was what the job was about. They had been advised to focus on the medical staff at all the local hospitals in the areas as the murder victim was also a doctor, a young recently qualified doctor. The cause of death was the same as the Smythe murder and the murder weapon had never been found.

Chapter 20

Henry was late coming home from his clinic and was tired. These past few months were taking a toll on his health, he thought. It was getting more difficult to relax. Only for Viv being able to babysit, life would be more complicated, he knew. As he came into his house, he could hear the children laughing and chattering in the sitting room. He looked in and found the three of them curled up on the sofa, watching an old children's movie, which though old, was still hilarious to watch and was a favourite of Mark's. They had a big bowl of popcorn on the table in front of them and there seemed to be a lot on the floor, as well! They waved at him cheerfully and Mark said, 'Dad, come and watch this with us, the next bit is really great!'

'I'll just go and get my dinner first, if you don't mind, I'm starving. I just hope that you have left me some.'

He went out to the kitchen and found his dinner in the oven. He ate it solitarily and listened to the roars of laughter coming from the sitting room. He smiled to himself and thought how adaptable children were and was grateful for that.

Later when the children were in bed, he thanked Viv as they had a glass of wine. She leaned back on the sofa and told him what lovely children he had and that she really enjoyed being with them.

'Honestly Viv? I would have thought that you had better things to do, than babysit for me. Children can be quite draining, I think. So many questions and never quite satisfied with the answers. There is always a "but why?" Explanations exhaust me,' he said smiling at her.

'No Henry, they are wonderful, if full of questions. I would love to have had children,' she said wistfully.

'Was there never anyone special in your life, Viv?' Henry asked gently.

'Once upon a time, there was. Alas, it fizzled out, Henry.' Viv sighed and put down her glass and rose to her feet.

'Time to go, tomorrow is a busy day, lots of patients. But after tomorrow it is easier, I will be free any time you need me to come over.'

She went and got her coat. Henry helped her to put it on and saw her to the hall door. He paused and said shyly, 'I am really very grateful Viv, for all the time you put into my kids. I don't know how I can ever repay you.'

She stood on tiptoe and kissed his cheek. 'No need, Henry, they fulfill a need in me, and we get along quite nicely.'

When she had left, Henry watched the news on television but soon discovered that he was not absorbing it. He found himself thinking of Viv. He thought that she would be a wonderful mother. What did he feel about her? He wondered if he could ever feel attracted to her but knew in his heart, that there was no chemistry there. He could communicate with her wonderfully and they both were interested in similar things and she was highly articulate and intelligent. She was a strong woman, well able to stand up for herself in a male dominated profession. She was the direct opposite to poor Lizzie. Was it that she was too strong, and he felt intimidated? No, that surely was male arrogance. Did he seek women that he could dominate? He did not know the answer to that. His problem with his attitude to women all originated with Linda. It was all her doing when she seduced him. He sighed as he rose and switched off the television. It would be so convenient if he was attracted to her. He knew is his heart that she would be willing to marry him. But was it the children that attracted her or was she also attracted to him? He sighed again and left the room to go to bed.

The next week was a hellish one for Henry. The police requested another meeting at the station. The children's DNA was only partially matching the prints at the professor's house. They were going to request an exhumation of his wife's body. Henry was floored and angry. How could they do this? It was because of the confession and the tie, he was told. His wife was implicated in a murder and they had to find out if she had entered the premises. He felt helpless and appealed to his solicitor. It was out of their hands, he was told.

Henry kept his head down and tried to concentrate on his work. He told nobody about the exhumation order and hoped it would all go away. He attended one of the meetings of his ADD parents. He enjoyed these meetings, informal and friendly as they were. It was while he was there chatting, that he realised why he liked these meetings, infrequent as they were. He usually met with a lot of mothers with ADD children. There was one mother particularly, that he always had time for; Susan was a single mother of a mildly autistic child, a little boy of four years of age. She was a physiotherapist at the same hospital where he worked, although their paths never seemed to cross. He always sought her out and inquired about her boy. She was a cheerful woman, always smiling and very helpful to the other mothers too. She was quietly spoken and a very good listener. Henry found himself wanting to talk more to her and over tea, asked if she would go out some night with him for a meal? When she hesitated, he realised that she would have to get a babysitter.

'I have a better idea,' he said. 'Why don't you and Jack have an outing to the zoo with my two and me, and then we could all have supper, wherever the kids want?' He waited hopefully.

'That sounds good, Henry. Jack loves the zoo and it would be like a party, wouldn't it? He just loves parties!'

Henry was thrilled and went home elated. Ivy was still there when he arrived. Viv was out of town for a few days as her uncle had become unwell. He had almost forgotten about the exhumation, how strange! Later in bed, he of course thought about it and all the anxieties returned. Poor Lizzie. He hoped she was happy in the next world and unaware of the indignities heaped on her body and name. As a Christian he did believe, although at times it was a struggle, especially since Lizzie died.

The week continued with Henry edgy and tense, waiting for a call from the police station. He rang himself, as he could not rest, to find out what was happening. He was told that tests had been conducted but the results would take some time. They were apologetic and seemed almost human, for once.

Later at the hospital, he got a call from Viv to say her uncle had died. She was upset and asked Henry if he could attend the funeral, as there was no one else, except her. Of course, Henry was sympathetic and said he would go to the funeral, which was the following day. He arranged cover for the morning and afternoon clinics and travelled to the town where the funeral would take place. There was a small gathering of staff and a few mobile patients from the old folk's home, where Viv's uncle had spent so many years. There was a small reception later in the local hotel and Henry got to meet some of the people present. Later, Viv expressed her gratitude for his presence.

'Viv, after all you have done for me, it was a very small thing I did,' Henry said.

'Well, it meant an awful lot to me Henry, and I really appreciated it,' she said smiling.

Viv had to stay for a couple of days and see the solicitor who was looking after her uncle's business affairs. She had arranged a week's leave. She hoped everything was alright with Henry. He did not want to upset her with news about how the police has requested an exhumation order. She had enough on her plate, poor girl.

'Will you stay and have an early dinner with me?'

Henry did not have the heart to refuse. He rang Ivy and she agreed to stay on.

It was much later, and Viv had quite a lot to drink. Henry was very careful, he had to drive home. Viv did not notice that he was not drinking. She became very maudlin and weepy. Her uncle was her only connection with family and now he was gone. She was now alone in the world. Henry murmured sympathetically and said he understood.

'Life is so hard, Henry. I may look as though I have everything, but in fact I have very little. Plenty of money yes, but at the end of the day, what does it mean? I cannot have children, and after all, they are so important to a woman, don't you agree?' Tears rolled down her cheeks.

Henry wiped her face with his handkerchief. 'How do you know that, Viv, have you ever tried?' He was a bit uncomfortable with the turn in the conversation but was also curious.

'Henry, I was once pregnant, and I lost it. I was told I could never have a baby.' She sobbed.

'Viv, there are many treatments now and miscarriage is not what it used to be, even multi-miscarriages.'

Viv downed her drink. Turning to Henry, she whispered, 'Yes, I know Henry, but they ruined my uterus, so I can't.'

Shocked, Henry replied, 'What do you mean, Viv? Who ruined your uterus?'

She hiccupped and replied, 'The abortionist my boyfriend insisted I visit.' She poured another glass of wine and gulped half of it.

Henry was appalled and could not think what to say. He wiped away the tears that were coursing down Viv's face and put his arm around her, shushing her. He gently asked a few more questions and Viv told him all about it. She had become pregnant when she was a young doctor and had been so happy. She was in love, after all. She believed this man was the man of her dreams and that they would live happily ever after. How mistaken she was! When she knew that he was seeing someone else, she confronted him with her news and he had told her that she could get rid of it, for all he cared. He had a career to get on with and he was not ready for marriage and fatherhood. He had plans to go far in his career and she was also a clever girl and would go far in her career and yes, they had had a good time for a while, now it was over.

Viv was ready to collapse so Henry helped her up the stairs to the room she was staying in and put the woman to bed. He hoped that she would remember nothing of this in the morning. He would never forget it and wondered how Viv had coped with this awful tragedy in her early life.

It was midnight when at last Henry reached home and Ivy was asleep on the sofa in the sitting room. She woke up as he entered the room. Henry apologised profusely and insisted that Ivy go to bed up in the bedroom that used to be Lizzie's. He would hear no denial and insisted that she stay in bed in the morning and not dare get up to see the children off to school. He would do that, and she must rest. He told her that he did not know how they would cope without her. She admitted that she would not object to a lie in.

Next morning, he told the children about Viv's uncle dying. They asked about Viv's family and where her parents were, and did she have brothers and sisters? They felt sad for her to learn that she had nobody else in the world.

To cheer them up, he then told them about the planned visit to the zoo on Sunday next. He told them about the little boy, Jack, that they were going to meet and his mother, Susan. He explained a little about Autism and how it affected people. Now they were totally distracted from the sad news and highly excited about the outing planned, especially when they heard that they would all be dining out. There was a lovely restaurant just across the road from the zoo entrance, which was very popular with all the visitors to the zoo. Henry went to work and tried to put Viv's story out of his mind. He hoped that she was too drunk to remember her confession. How embarrassing it would be for them both, if she recalled her conversation with him.

Chapter 21

Detectives Jones and Miller returned to headquarters exhausted after a week's digging about in the south. They had learned some interesting facts and reported to their boss, or 'Guv', as he was known. They had all the details of the murdered doctor and where he worked, the different hospitals he had worked in but unfortunately, nobody remembered him from back then as most of the junior doctors had moved on. Only one person they asked about was remembered. That was Professor Smythe. She had been lecturing in the area around that time, in various hospitals and at the University. She was known to be a brilliant teacher and many doctors sought a position studying under her. Nobody was very forthcoming about being compromised by the same teacher.

'But here's the thing, Guv', said Miller. 'She had a flat that she offered to people who were seeking accommodation and seemingly, when she moved to the Midlands, here, the same offer applied in her new house, which is the one she was living in when she was murdered.'

Jones told the people in the room that the professor was very generous, and it was not just males that stayed there. Any junior doctor arriving without accommodation could stay there while they looked around the area for a suitable place. They were all earning, so it was not like they were looking for free accommodation, although it was known that the professor did not expect remuneration at all. A different side to the woman, all agreed. Most of those doctors staying at the accommodation she offered, were interested in psychiatric services or psychology, or university jobs.

The boss suggested that they start looking at any students from back then, that may have surfaced here or nearby. It had to be someone with a big grudge. Perhaps a male, who did not cooperate or did not get a reference? The hopes of an early solution seemed as far away as ever to the two men, who had gone south so eagerly. Answers come so easily, they thought, especially on television series.

They were then told the news that Mrs. Dukes' DNA was analysed and proved beyond a doubt that she was in the professor's house. The prints on the hall door and handle of the sitting room, plus another on the desk, behind which the body lay.

That floored them. The height and weight of the suspect was so unlikely to be able to carry out a vicious stabbing was a mystery to them. The boss said it did not mean that she was alone. There was no trace of Henry's DNA, except for the tie, just Lizzie's and the other mystery prints, which, by the way, were not found in the room of the murder, but in the basement flat and the interconnecting door to the professor's quarters on the first floor.

They sat and thought about it and then recapped all the information that they had gathered so far. Jones enumerated the various points and Miller enlarged on them. Point one, the woman was severely depressed and on medication, as well as being almost an alcoholic, although that could not be proved. Then the next point caused a bit of discussion; the confession of the woman, complete with details about the tie being put around the victim's neck. Usually a confession was all that was needed, wasn't it? The Guv pointed out that the suspect was right-handed, and the pathologist was adamant that the murderer was left-handed. The final point made, was Grace's statement about the mother's suicide, due to the same type of depression, although *that* poor woman was not on any medication. Then the fact, discovered later, that the suspect was receiving anonymous phone calls for years before, which distressed her. Why had nobody believed the woman and complained? So, three people showing different aspects of the case, a bit of a jigsaw, Miller said, that needed joining up. There would be other results to come, which were still being tested in the laboratory which might shed some light on the suspect's health, although suicide was a much more probable belief now. It could be guilt after committing the murder.

It was decided that nothing would be communicated to Henry at this point, except the fact that his wife had been in the house and that only, if he enquired again. They might need him in for further questioning later. In the meantime, they were told to get out the spades and keep digging. Miller, and Jones, thought that it might be profitable to ask some questions at the university where the professor lectured and set up a confidential phone line, some people might be shy or sensitive about personal information being bandied about.

The murder weapon had never been found and now that it was proved that Lizzie was in the house, the Guv said he thought it was time the Dukes' house was searched, but not until all the lab results were in.

Chapter 22

Sunday dawned bright and sunny. Father and children returned from church in great excitement. Henry was really looking forward to being with Susan and Jack and having his children meet both. He had prayed that morning that all would go well, and if there was to be any future for him, that it would be with Susan.

They met at the zoo car park at two o'clock. The three children could hardly wait and practically ran through the zoo entrance. Susan looked relaxed and happy and smiled at Henry as they chatted. They were able to have an uninterrupted conversation most of the time, as Jack immediately attached himself to Mark. They wandered all over the place, visiting the different areas. The reptile house was of course a horrifying but hypnotic place for them. Jack was the only one not seen to display any fear of the creatures. At one end, a keeper had taken out a snake for the children around to admire, a harmless one of course. It was interesting to see how most of the children backed away, especially the bigger bolder types, who normally would not show fear of anyone or anything. Jack was the exception, he edged forward and put out his hand to stroke the reptile, as the keeper had invited them to do. Mark, in awe, gradually moved in beside him and nervously put his hand out. Jack turned and smiled at him.

'So soft', he said, as he continued to gently stroke the creature. The keeper gradually lowered the reptile down to Jack's shoulder and the next thing, it was around his neck. There was a horrified gasp from the back of the crowd of children. Jack did not even flinch although Mark moved away quickly. Then it was time for the snake to go back into his glass cage.

The monkey area proved a very happy place for them all. Henry and Susan sat on a bench where they could observe the children going from cage to cage, giggling and having fun.

Henry learned that Susan had an apartment on Church Street, which was a fifteen-minute walk to Jack's playschool. She thought that he would be able for main-stream school as his autism was very mild. Henry thought so too. Her mother lived very close by and was a great support to her, collecting Jack from school and minding him until Susan was finished work. She did not have much time for hobbies these days, she told Henry, but hoped to take up violin again when Jack was older. Her great love was music. They chatted about the demands of children on single parents and Henry told her about Ivy and what a godsend she was.

After hours of walking around and generally enjoying themselves, the children suddenly discovered that they were starving. They walked back to the entrance and towards the restaurant beside the car park. Inside, there followed a quick debate on what they wanted to eat; pizza, burger or fish and chips? Jack knew exactly what he wanted, pizza! Mark agreed, and Marianne and the two adults went for burger and salad. Marianne told Susan about the piano exam she was now preparing for, having done one, so far. Susan told her that she had played violin and had done some exams too. They chatted away happily and Henry, looking at other families around them, longed to be just like them again. If it happened, he vowed, it would be different this time. Work would not take first place, his family would. He would adapt his hours to make sure he had time to spend with them. He was in a little daydream of his own, when someone approached their table. Looking up he was surprised to see Viv. She looked happy and bright and smiled at them all. Henry introduced her to Susan and Jack. She told them that she was here with 'her teenagers', nodding over in the direction of a table where two glowering teens sat, unsmiling.

'Have you been at the zoo too, Viv?' Susan smiled up at Viv.

'Oh no! They would consider themselves too grown-up for that! I just bring them here for a meal some weekends, to give their poor mother a break, they would wreck anybody's head!'

Henry explained to Susan that Viv working in the Maternity Hospital on Bridge Avenue but took an interest in troubled teens.

'Very admirable, Viv. I'm not sure I could do that. My Jack keeps me fully occupied.'

Viv said she would be back at work the coming week and if he needed a babysitter, just let her know. She smiled at them all and went back to her sulky two. Then it was time to go home, bedtime for Jack and the other two looked tired out too. They said they would do this again as it was such fun. Henry was desperate not to let the opportunity slip without making a future date. He suggested that as the weather was warming up, they might like a barbeque in his back garden. Susan said that sounded wonderful and a date was set up for the following Saturday afternoon.

Henry returned home a contented and happy man. For a whole afternoon, he had never thought once about the police inquiry or anything else. Marianne was interested in Susan and her violin playing. He joked that they might learn to play duets. They both liked Jack, and Mark would not stop talking about the bravery of the four-year old with the snake. He would never have got so close to the snake if it had not been for Jack, and yes, snakes did feel soft and not at all slimy as you would suppose.

The week progressed as normal and Henry was busy. He also spent a while just looking at his files and diary and wondered how he could streamline his life a bit more. He had little time for research anymore and he missed this. He thought about job opportunities and about whether it was time for a change. He must find time to discuss this with a couple of friends. He decided that one private clinic a week would be better for family life, not that it kept him very late, but he would like to be present to bring Mark to football and Marianne to athletics. He was a very absent father for those activities. In another few years they would not need him anyway, they would be totally independent. How would they see him when they were adult; what would their memories of his presence be? His own memories of his late father were all good. His dad had been a constant presence in his and Betts' life, always there and so supportive. It made him realise that he had not been at all like his father. He knew that this was, in part, because of his relationship with Lizzie and how the marriage had gradually broken down.

When he arrived home, he found Viv there with the children. She had brought Marianne to piano and then returned after the lesson with her, and let Ivy leave for home. Henry immediately thought of his good intentions. He could not even remember when Marianne's lesson was on! She stayed on, and they all had the dinner that Ivy had left in the oven, the shepherd's pie that Mark so loved. Afterwards the children went upstairs to their rooms to finish their homework.

Henry told Viv about his ideas for a new work schedule and being more a father. She laughed and said she understood exactly how he felt. A doctor's life was too busy, but she wished him well in trying to simplify it.

When she had left, he called the children down to chat and over cocoa and biscuits, he asked them to write out their weekly activity schedule and put it on the fridge.

'You must remind me each day, about your activities for that day so that I do not forget. I want to be here to bring you, when I can,' he explained.

'Dad, you don't have to worry about us,' Marianne said, 'Viv will always drop us.'

'It would be nice if you could, Dad,' said Mark, 'but Viv is a great help really.'

Henry felt a bit deflated at their lack of enthusiasm but knew in his heart that they had grown used to his not being there. He felt sad and wondered if things could ever change.

Saturday came and Henry and the two children went shopping for the barbeque. They knew what they wanted although Henry did not have any idea about how to do a barbeque.

'We need chicken pieces Dad and maybe a few sausages,' suggested Marianne.

'Don't forget ribs, Dad, I just love them, and they cook quickly. You might need some steak too for yourself and Susan.' Mark grinned up at him.

'And there must be baked potatoes and a big bowl of salad,' said Marianne.

'And how do you both know so much about barbeques, huh?' He was amazed by their knowledge. He and Lizzie never did a barbeque.

'Tommy's mum and Mum's friends used to do them and of course, Viv.' Mark relayed all this in a very grown-up voice.

'Well that's great then, both of you can organise it all and I can learn!' Henry was amused.

'Well, we know nothing about wine, so you will have to buy that. We are not allowed fizzy, so fruit juice, maybe, although Viv says that it is just as bad. She only lets us drink water.'

'But be sure to get crisps and some dips, Jack will like them.'

It was an educational outing for Henry and humbling. They knew so much, and he was totally ignorant. He enjoyed the outing and the shopping as much as the children. They had everything prepared by lunch time. They then pulled out the barbeque cooker, which was stored in the garage, practically brand new. Henry was glad to see that it was a gas cooker. He was worried about having to light a fire and how hot it should be. The gas cylinder was full, and he had matches. All was ready. He put a white wine in the fridge and had a red wine open, to breathe, as he explained to the children. There was garlic bread too and the potatoes were washed and ready to go into the oven.

Susan had arranged to come over at three o'clock. Jack had sports and games on Saturday morning and she always brought him to the library. There was a story-telling session every Saturday at noon, for an hour.

When they arrived at three, everything was well started, food would be ready to eat at three thirty. Henry felt very pleased with himself!

The children ran to open the door and welcomed Jack into their house. The child's eyes lit up when he saw the big back garden and swings. He ran straight onto one of them and Mark came up behind and began to push him. Marianne brought Susan up to see her digital piano and showed her the pieces that she was preparing. Susan suggested that sometime, she might bring her violin and play along with Marianne. This thrilled the girl.

The barbeque was a great success and the children did justice to all the food. After the meal, Mark took Jack up to his bedroom and showed him all his Lego and toys. Jack immediately began to make things with the Lego and Mark was surprised at how skillful he was.

Henry and Susan sat in the warm sunshine and chatted while Marianne cleared away the dishes and food, all this without being asked. Henry was very proud of her. When it got cooler, they went indoors, and a movie was found for them all to watch. Henry felt so relaxed with Susan and she seemed happy in his company. Marianne mentioned about what Susan said earlier, about coming and playing her violin. At about six o'clock the doorbell rang, and Mark ran out to answer it. It was Viv. She entered the sitting room and greeted them all. She had brought a bottle of wine with her and some treats for the children. She apologised for intruding but as she had been passing, thought she would say hello and wondered if Henry wanted to go out or if he needed her to babysit. She said if she had known they had visitors, she would not have come in.

Henry said not at all, it was always lovely to see her. Marianne said that there was some barbequed food left and asked if she could get her a plate, but Viv told them that she had already eaten. They chatted amiably for a time and then Susan stood up and said she must go, as Jack needed to be in bed early, especially after a day of excitement.

Henry saw her to the door and walked her to the roadway where her car was parked. He said that he would ring her during the coming week. She thanked him for the lovely day. Then Jack said, 'I want to come again and play with Mark. He's given me a box of Lego and he's going to be my best friend!'

Henry and Susan laughed, and Jack waved them off and returned to the house.

'What a lovely woman Susan is,' Viv said. 'And the little boy. Does she work fulltime at the hospital?'

'Yes, I think she does. She has a mother nearby, who helps her out with Jack. He is mildly autistic, you know.'

'He is very, very clever, Dad. You should see how fast he was able to make things with the Lego, much quicker than I could!'

Mark was very impressed. Then he went on to tell Viv about how brave Jack was with the snake at the zoo. She smiled at his enthusiasm.

Viv then asked Henry for his advice. Her uncle had left her the house that he used to live in, and she did not know whether she should rent it out or sell it.

'I don't know if I want the stress and bother of renting it. Tenants can be a bother, can't they?'

Henry advised her to check with an estate agent and find out what the market was like and what rents were in that area. After that, she would just have to think about it and then come to a decision.

'You could get a letting agent to manage it all for you. They take care of everything for a price, maintenance and repairs and all of that. You would not have to get involved at all.'

She rose to go and said that she would think about it. She told him that she appreciated his advice and 'for being such a good and reliable friend.'

Henry was grateful that nothing was mentioned about her tearful confession and wondered whether she had remembered it the next morning. He hoped that she hadn't.

Chapter 23

Susan was very happy these days. Her mother noticed her joyful spirit and enquired who the man was! Mothers had too much intuition, Susan felt. She admitted that she was seeing someone, it was true, but it was very early days. She explained about Henry and his children and how they had gone to the zoo and had a barbeque and that the children had all got on very well. She told her mother about Henry being a widower and what a tragic life the family had experienced. Her mother told her to keep her head about her and not fall in love out of pity. That would never work, she told her daughter. They both laughed at that. Her mother was the softest creature alive, Susan thought. When Susan's relationship had broken down, her mother was so sympathetic but practical too. She had liked the lad but thought that he was immature and not ready for responsibility. She was proved right when Susan got pregnant.

Susan had heard the rumours around the hospital when Lizzie had died. Everyone thought that it was suicide. Her depression had been continual for a very long time. Having met the two children, she was surprised and happy to find them so normal and well-adjusted. She wondered if Henry would think it forward of her if she invited him to a function. She had an invitation to the opening of an art exhibition later in the week and could take someone with her. Would he be interested in art, she wondered? It was only a two-hour event with cheese and wine thrown in. She decided that she would ring him. Her mother would babysit for her, she knew.

Henry was busy looking up new positions in the medical journals when his phone rang. He was like a young boy when he discovered it was Susan. Of course, he would love to go to the opening, and he was interested in art. He made a note in his diary for the following Friday night.

He would check with Viv and if she was busy, perhaps Ivy would be able. If she wasn't, he was not sure what to do. It was time to find an independent babysitter. Their previous babysitter had gone on to university. He would ask Kate or maybe Sarah. Surely they would have a babysitter that they could recommend. As the day progressed, he reached the conclusion that he must ask Lizzie's friends about a babysitter. It would not be fair to always expect Viv to be available. No time like the present, he thought. I'll call in to Kate tonight.

It was Tuesday night and he remembered Mark's football and Marianne's athletics. He was proud of himself. The children were surprised too, and they all headed off after dinner. The neighbours were there too, with their children. Henry brought up the subject of babysitting with Kate as they stood watching their sons at football training. Kate told him about the wonderful sitter that they had, a young woman who lived nearby and was very experienced. She recommended her and thought that if they both needed a sitter at the same time, that she would have a friend who would oblige. She gave him an idea about how much to pay her. He was quite shocked! He never knew babysitting was so expensive! Kate laughed at him and told him that up to now, he had been spoiled. He left the sports ground with the girl's number and rang it when he came home. The young lady agreed to come and babysit on Friday night from seven to nine. He later told the two children and looked at him as if he was from another planet.

'Why do we need a babysitter, Dad, won't Viv do it?' Mark was quite indignant.

'It's not really fair to expect Viv to spend her time babysitting, now is it? Now and again I'm sure she doesn't mind, but nobody likes being taken for granted.' Henry reasoned with him.

'But Viv really likes us, Dad,' Marianne remonstrated. 'We are used to her and we know that she likes being here with us. We don't know this new lady. What if we don't like her?'

Henry explained that it would be for two hours only and that they would be in their rooms doing their homework or reading, so it would not affect them at all. He could feel their antagonism. He thought that it was a pity that Lizzie and himself had never availed themselves of a babysitting service years ago. The whole idea now was foreign to them and he hoped that they would not show their resentment to the poor girl on Friday.

Friday came and Henry was home at six o'clock for dinner with the children. They were sitting watching television when he came down from having a shower. They did not look at all happy.

'Now listen, you two, I expect you to act your age for the next two hours and not give this girl any hassle. She minds your friends when their parents go out. You don't want her giving a bad report to them, do you?'

Mark rolled his eyes and said, 'I just hope that this won't happen too often.'

The doorbell rang and Henry moved to open it, looking at them warningly over his shoulder.

The girl who entered the house was extremely friendly and chatty and before Henry had left, he knew that Mark was won over. They were all chatting earnestly when he said goodbye.

The art exhibition was held at the county museum. It was well attended as it was a local artist who was making his debut. There were photographers there, probably from the local and national newspapers, clicking away. Susan looked stunning in a green sheath dress of very soft and clinging material. Henry could hardly take his eyes off her. They walked slowly around viewing the paintings, most of which were abstract. Henry could not really concentrate on them with Susan so close to him. She asked him what sort of art he liked, and he vaguely said he thought all art offered something to the viewer. She was not too taken by some of the work, it was a bit garish, she thought. He agreed. There were some pictures, however, that were powerful and pulling and he thought that he could live with one or two. Susan agreed but said she could not live with the prices requested! They moved around laughing and sipping their glass of wine.

It was over, all too soon, for Henry. As they left the building and crossed the road to where Susan had parked her car, Henry pulled her to him and as she lifted her face, he gently kissed her. It lasted a long time. 'I've wanted to do that for some time,' he said, smiling down at her.

'I have wanted it too,' replied Susan.

'What would you say to a trip to the seaside with the kids, my mother has a holiday home by the sea. A weekend, say?'

Susan sighed, 'I could be tempted by that! Jack loves the sea and so do I.'

'Let me check my diary and see if there is a long weekend on the horizon, and we'll plan it, ok?'

They both parted with a new dream in their hearts.

Chapter 24

The weekend chosen for the beach visit could not have been better. It was a long weekend and the sun shone all day, every day. The children spent hours playing in the sand, making castles and swimming at regular intervals to cool off. There were trips to the shop for ice cream and one evening they went to a nearby recreation park where there were pony rides and a carousel. Every night the children went to bed, tired out. Henry felt that he was getting to know Susan and they were taking the relationship slowly. They both had experienced a loving union and knew true love could not be rushed and knowing the individual was so important. Susan especially, was not going to be rushed into anything. Her commitment to her son was the most important thing in her life as were Henry's children to him, she believed. They were happy to explore each other's minds and past experiences. Henry wanted Susan to meet Grace sometime soon. He felt they would get on well together and as he considered Lizzie's family also his, he wanted Susan to be part of that too. Susan told him all about Jack's father and how disappointed she had been in that relationship. Now, she felt that it was all for the best, as Jack's father would never have been able to cope with him, or any child, she thought. She considered herself fortunate not to have been married to him. She listened when Henry told her of his perfect marriage to Lizzie and then how it all unravelled with postnatal depression which just never went away.

They went on walks with the three children most days, before dinner. Marianne chatted away to Susan and seemed comfortable with her. She had done well in her piano exam and she was looking forward to her next one. Susan told her that she would be soon going back to playing her violin. Seeing how hard Marianne had worked had started her thinking about it. She suggested getting together now and again for some simple duet playing.

Mark and Jack had fun fishing about in the rock pools and examining everything they found. Jack was very interested in all living creatures and always made Mark return their finds to the water. He was a bit nervous of the sea however, and it took a lot of coaxing to get him to go in up to his knees in the water. Mark had great patience with him and by the time the weekend came to an end, Jack was a lot more confident and was lying down at the edge of the water and letting the waves lap over him. Susan was thrilled to see his progress as she knew he was frightened of the sea although loving the beach.

Marianne, more observant than her brother, noticed the way her father and Susan looked at each other and thought her father was falling in love. She was a bit shocked at first, when it dawned on her. Thinking about it over a couple of days, she found that she liked the idea, because she liked Susan and saw that she made Henry happy. She had never seen her father smile or laugh as much. She also liked Jack and knew that her brother did too. Jack brought out a caring and protective side in Mark, which she had never seen before.

Henry also noticed his children's reaction to Susan and Jack and felt a huge sense of relief. He could not have a relationship with anyone if it brought unhappiness or antagonism to his children. He would contact Grace soon and have a chat and hope a combined visit up north could happen before winter came.

On their last afternoon, after they tidied and locked the house, they paid a visit to the nearby town. Henry wanted to get Ivy a present and Susan wanted to get her mother something. The children were given some money to buy whatever they wanted and lots of sticks of peppermint rock were purchased for friends. They had their final ice cream in the seaside café where they had enjoyed some fish and chip suppers. Then it was back into the car for the long drive home.

They stopped on the way, at Henry's mother's house to return the key, and Betts had a lovely supper waiting for them. Iris, Henry's mother had been delighted to meet Susan and Jack. The past few years had been sad for them all; first with her husband dying and then poor Lizzie. She was hopeful again for Henry, that he had found someone to share his life. She had been very blessed with a happy life and she knew how Henry had suffered when Lizzie had been unwell.

All three children were sound asleep when they arrived home. Henry dropped off Susan and carried Jack into their house. Then he proceeded with his sleeping two. He felt refreshed and ready for work again. He thought that people should take breaks more often from work and then felt guilty for not doing so when Lizzie was alive.

In work the following week he met his two friends and they suggested that they repeat their almost forgotten night out and jazz experience! Henry was all for it and they arranged for the following Friday night. The babysitter was booked, and Mark did not seem to object this time.

Henry had seen a couple of job advertisements in the medical journals and intended discussing them with the two lads. He remembered his last trip and losing his phone, so he made sure he left it in the car this time.

They had a meal in the pub first and a good natter. One of the other doctors was into research and thought the job at the university might suit Henry. The other one thought that Henry would be mad to give up his position at the hospital, seeing as how popular he was. Henry said that he thought it would be ideal if he could split the two. His friends thought that would be the best of both worlds, if it was possible. They thought that he should approach both departments and discuss it and see what they would think of a part time psychiatrist at the hospital and a part time lecturer at the university. He could only try, he thought.

They went on to the jazz club and being Friday night, it was again very crowded. Henry had never known that jazz was so popular in this town. They found a corner, not too near the music, they also wanted to chat and have a gossip too. About eleven, Henry was thinking about leaving when a huge crowd of people came through the door. As they congregated around the bar, the noise level was mighty and his friends nodded at each other and said, "Time, gentlemen". They all got up together and tried to edge towards the door. Henry leading, was almost there when someone grabbed his arm and said, 'Hello, stranger!' Looking around, Henry was surprised to see Viv there, with a bunch of girls that he recognised from the various departments in the hospital. He greeted her and she nodded at the bunch of girls and said, 'Hen party, wouldn't you know?' He laughed and hoped that they would enjoy themselves. One of the other girls, from his office, said, 'Oh we will doctor, we love it here it!'

They finally got away and headed for their cars. Nobody had drunk very much that night, certainly not Henry. He was happy that he had discussed his job options with the boys. He would do what they suggested and try to get a job-sharing position. Quite a few people were doing that nowadays and it was certainly a great help for female professionals, trying to juggle family life and a career.

The babysitting was working out well and the two seemed happy enough with Jean, the young student. The fact that she brought along her books to study also impressed them. She was studying to be a vet and Mark was full of questions about what she had to learn.

Viv called in during the week. She had heard from Henry about Marianne's good piano results. She arrived with gift wrapped box one afternoon. Marianne was so thrilled when she opened the box and found a lovely winter jacket with hood in her favourite colour, pink! She thanked Viv and went into the kitchen to show Ivy, who thought that it was lovely too. Ivy offered Viv a coffee and all three females sat in the kitchen drinking coffee and discussing what bargains the local shops had on offer. When Mark appeared, he immediately told Viv that he had something for her and she went into the sitting room with him, where he presented her with a stick of rock. Marianne following, said that she had the same thing for her too.

'I had better eat them slowly and carefully, so I don't pull out my fillings!'

The children laughed and said, 'Dad told us the same.'

Viv asked them, when had they been at the seaside? They then proceeded to tell her about their weekend away in Granny's house by the sea, with Susan and Jack and what a great time they all had. They were both quite bronzed from the sun and sea air. Mark then had to leave as Tommy called for him to go out and play. Viv asked Marianne if she had started her new pieces yet and Marianne showed her the new book. She mentioned that Susan was going to bring her violin and that they would try to play some easy duets together. Viv thought that people who could make music were very lucky.

'Why don't you learn, Viv, it's never too late, you know, you're not that old.'

Viv laughed and agreed that it was never too late to learn anything.

'I have something sort of private to tell you, Viv, but you must not tell anyone.'

She looked inquiringly at Viv, who crossed her heart and put her finger on her lips, still smiling.

'Well, Viv, I suspect that Dad is falling in love with Susan, what do you think of that?'

She grinned over at Viv, sitting on the sofa.

Viv said carefully, 'I think that is lovely, Marianne. Your dad deserves some happiness, don't you agree?'

Marianne nodded her head vigorously. 'I'm not sure if Susan is falling in love with Dad though, I know that they get on very well.'

Ivy put her head around the door just then, and asked Viv if she was in a hurry to leave?

Viv said not at all. Ivy's daughter had an appointment at the local clinic and Ivy had been asked to babysit. It was sudden and she hadn't known this morning before Henry left for work.

Viv told her that she was free, and it was no problem.

When Henry returned from work, the children were finishing their homework and had eaten their dinner. All was calm and quiet. Marianne showed her father her new jacket and he admired it, at the same time telling Viv, that she was like a fairy godmother, spoiling them.

Chapter 25

Henry was a new man these days. He felt twenty years younger and even the children noticed a difference in him. Ivy was quietly happy for she could see that the doctor was walking with a lighter step and the sad lines around his mouth seemed to be disappearing. So, it was a shock to his system when the police contacted him again. He was to report to the station whenever was convenient. He cut short his afternoon clinic and drove down to the station. He was beginning to get a sick feeling in his stomach whenever he saw the station. He was shown into a room where the detectives Miller and Jones were already seated.

They came straight to the point as usual. He was told that his wife's presence in the house of the murder victim was now without doubt. Her DNA was found in three different places. Henry was shocked and knew then, that what his wife had told him was true. He just had not wanted to believe it.

'I thought you said the murder was committed by a left-handed person?'

'That is true, so there was another person involved, doctor.'

'It is too weird. Do you mean that my wife conspired to commit this murder with someone else?

Someone, whom she *knew*? They *both* conspired to carry this out, *together*? I find that preposterous!'

Jones took up a piece of paper and handed it to Henry. It was a form from a laboratory, stating a list of chemicals and toxins found in body tissue of the recently exhumed body of Mrs. Lizzie Dukes. Henry could not make much sense of what was on the form.

'What is all this about?' Henry gave the form back to the men across the desk.

They then explained that analysis of some tissue had shown a high level of different chemicals, some very strong psychotic drugs and other very strong sedatives. Could he explain why his wife would have such an amount of medication taken? Henry shook his head and said that he could not. She had been on medication for years but only what were usual amounts, for postnatal depression.

'Doctor Dukes, did your wife commit suicide, in your opinion?' Miller leaned back in his chair and stared across at Henry.

'I really do not know. I had hoped not, but seeing that, makes me wonder. Her mother died by suicide you know.'

'It would be mighty convenient if she did, wouldn't you say?' Jones remarked.

'What do you mean by that, may I ask?' Henry was growing impatient.

'It would mean that whoever the other person was, now remains unknown, doesn't it?'

Miller threw his pen on the table. 'The secret dies with your wife, doctor, doesn't it?'

Jones leaned across the table and asked, 'Doctor, did you prescribe extra medication for your wife?'

'Of course not. I would never do that, and Lizzie would never ask. She had her own doctor who was also a friend.'

'Did you murder Linda Smythe while your wife looked on?' Jones and Miller were directing very hostile looks at Henry, who looked very shocked and noticeably paled.

Then they suddenly changed tack and Miller sighed, and said in a much more friendly tone of voice, 'Doctor Dukes, it is completely understandable why you would want to kill this person, between seducing you and torturing you wife with nasty phone calls, totally understandable.'

Henry finally found his voice and retorted, 'Understandable maybe, except that I did not kill anyone and neither did my wife, as far I understand it. She was not left-handed, and I am, but to kill someone! I do not think I would be capable either.'

'But your wife was so disturbed and did not really want to go away for treatment, did she?'

'No, but I think that she was coming around to the idea that it was the best thing for her to do. She was due to be accessed the day after she died. But you know that already,' he replied bitterly.

'Did you murder your wife, doctor, after her confession and knowing that she was implicated? Did you administer a powerful dose of drugs, thinking that all this investigation would be then unnecessary? Is her medication still at the house?'

Henry shook his head, feeling numb. 'I did not kill Lizzie, I loved her. I don't know about any medications left. Her sister took care of all that. I can ask her what she did with it. I have not seen any medication around, but then I have not looked either.'

Henry was shell-shocked, first his wife was a suspect, then he was and now they were accusing him of murdering his wife too? It was a Kafkaesque scenario.

Then they sprang the awful surprise on him: they had a warrant to search his house. He was dazed at how things were happening, so fast and without any warning. He never remembered leaving the station later. Ivy met him in the kitchen and was shocked by his appearance. She made him sit down and made him a cup of tea and listened to what he had been subjected to.

The search was conducted that afternoon. Henry collected the children from school, and they went to the park. He told them that he needed some fresh air and thought they could go to a movie after. The children were glad of course, but something about their father's demeanor made them feel unsettled. They felt that there was something wrong with him.

Marianne suddenly remembered that her piano lesson was that evening. Henry was in near despair. While they were walking ahead of him, he rang the house and spoke to Ivy. The men were now upstairs, having been downstairs and going through every cupboard and drawer they could find. She was not her usual placid self but was very annoyed and upset. Henry explained that he had to bring the children home as Marianne had a lesson. Then he had an idea. He would ring Viv and ask her to bring Marianne's music books from her room and meet them at the teacher's house. Ivy said that she would get the books ready for Viv to pick up.

Marianne was surprised and pleased to see Viv at the teacher's house and thanked her for bringing the books too. Then Viv suggested that they all go for supper to the pizza place after her lesson, the two children were happy with that. Henry kept ringing Ivy to see how things were going. At last, he received a call from Ivy, before they went out to eat; the police were gone. Henry slumped in relief. Later back at the house, Henry had a quick look around. Everything seemed back to normal, no mess, as he had expected. Poor Ivy must have tidied it all up. He did not imagine that the police would be worried about leaving stuff lying around.

Henry was exhausted. Viv poured him a whisky and brought it in to the sitting room to him. He told her that he had really believed it was all over, and now, he was back to square one. He believed that Lizzie had been in the house, the DNA proved it, and it must have been suicide after all. Then he told her that he had been asked if he had murdered Linda. He was now a suspect, he told Viv.

Viv told Henry to get some rest, if that was possible. She would be in touch with him later in the week. No matter what happens, she said, they have no proof that Lizzie was involved with the murder and he should now try and relax. It would now, after all this time, be put to bed and the police would leave him alone.

Henry had a broken sleep, he could not rest and twisted and turned. He remembered how he had woken to hear Lizzie screaming and found her in such a state. Her mind must have been in turmoil, he thought. Who had she been in touch with? Did she discuss her hatred with someone who decided to help her kill Linda? Had she watched the woman die? On and on the questions rolled out, he could not stop them. What about the children, when they later asked questions about their mother? How could he answer them? Towards dawn, he suddenly remembered Grace. A feeling of peace descended on him and he knew that she would come down immediately if he asked her. What a blessing it would be to have that woman here!

Grace arrived, promptly as usual and was concerned when she saw the state that Henry was in. When the children were in bed, she heard the whole story from him and listened in silence. When he had finished, Grace sighed.

'The idea of you being a suspect is ridiculous Henry. They must be desperate to blame somebody. I'm afraid that we have to accept that Lizzie took her own life, Henry, there can be other explanation, can there?'

Henry thought the same, sadly. 'Grace, it still doesn't explain why she was there, at Linda's house, nor does it tell us who killed the woman. Did she watch the murderer or help him? God knows, I can't make head nor tail of the whole mess!'

'I am only now understanding how my father felt, when my mother died. He just could not get his head around it either, he said. He could not tell us either, at that stage as we were too young. It was only later that he shared his sorrow and pain with us.' Grace wiped her eyes.

'That's the awful thing about suicide, it leaves so many questions that will always remain unanswered for those left behind,' agreed Henry.

Grace stayed for the week and gradually Henry felt that life might be returning to normal. There was no more word from the police, which he felt grateful for. The children were thrilled to have Grace with them and started to plan their next summer holiday at the farm. They took Grace to the park every day after school and on Sunday they drove out to nearby woods for a walk and a picnic. She listened to Marianne playing the piano and told her that she was very good indeed. One evening Viv called and was delighted to meet Grace and catch up on the news and various things of interest. They discussed Henry of course and what the poor man had endured, and Viv thought that the police must be rather desperate and clutching at straws in their efforts to solve Linda's killing.

Grace departed after the week, leaving Henry in much happier form and more optimistic. She issued Viv with an invitation to come up with Henry and the children, for a much needed, holiday, which Henry said they would take up.

There was no word from the police still, obviously they had found nothing of interest. Henry was relieved but also angry that it had happened at all. He intended to ring Susan as soon as possible and start again where they had left off. He looked at the calendar and saw that there would be a school midterm break in three weeks' time.

Work was the same as ever, very busy, but it was a relief to be able to concentrate again on something so normal. He rang Susan that night and mentioned about the half-term break and if she had any ideas of where she would like to visit? Susan asked him if he was sure he wanted them to go? Henry was puzzled and said that he could think of nothing better than to go with her and Jack. He knew his own two would be delighted at the thoughts of them all going. He wondered whether he had caught a hesitant vibe in her voice, as he finished the call. He felt unsettled after it. Was Susan changing her mind about a future with him and why. They had been so happy at the seaside and they were on the same wavelength, it seemed to Henry. Suddenly he realised just how much he wanted Susan and Jack in his and his children's lives. Perhaps he was mistaken. He decided to arrange to see Susan. He wondered how he could manage to 'accidently' bump into her at the hospital without being too obvious.

Chapter 26

Miller and Jones were working every hour that they could on this case. Their boss was demanding results and was anxious that the case would be sorted soon. He felt that it was all local and that all that was needed was strong motivation and lots of digging. Another trip down south was ordered. There had to be a connection with the murder of the young doctor down there with this one. It was so similar and there were the same prints at the scene.

Miller decided that he would travel down and asked Jones to go the university and ask more questions about Smythe's basement apartment and try and get a list of people who had resided there for no matter how short a period. Miller would try again to find out more about the murdered young doctor, his lifestyle, maybe try and contact his family although it was a long time ago.

Jones decided he would start by going back through records available, to find out the names of students working with Linda Smythe, over the past sixteen years or so, from the time that she had started working up here in the Midlands Psychiatric Hospital.

Miller struck gold first. Just by chance he discovered that the murdered Doctor Kumar's sister was also a doctor and working in Belgium. He was able to locate her through medical records and her name was on the inquest report. He contacted her through the hospital that she worked in and arranged a video link chat. He rang his partner Jones and gave him the news and was delighted that he also had made some progress. He had a list of some of the residents of the basement flat over the last sixteen years. Both men were feeling proud of themselves. They planned to be back at their office by the end of the week to compare notes and hoped the boss would have something to celebrate.

Henry rang Grace to ask her about any medication found in Lizzie's bathroom. Grace told him that she had only sorted out the clothes and that she had asked Viv to see to the medicines, in case they were of use. She did not think that there was much in the bathroom, from what she remembered. He had not been lucky to bump into Susan and decided to take the bull by the horns, regardless of what was thought of him. He was desperate to know if she was still interested in him. His life was in tatters he felt, and he looked on Susan as the only hope he had. Accordingly, he decided to call around to Susan's apartment and hoped that she would be there.

Having made the decision to go see her, he was suddenly afraid. He did not understand why he would be so nervous, like a teenager with a crush. He realised that it was because he was afraid that Susan would reject him. He did not know how he would cope with that. He sat in his car outside the compound. From here, he would see her ground floor apartment. It was in a well-built, two-storied building, comprised of twelve apartments. There were four such buildings, built in a square. There was a green square area in the middle, with trees and grass and a play area for children. There were several seating areas around and all in all, it looked very family oriented. The fact that none of the four buildings were more than two storied made it seem much more residential looking. He knew that these were expensive apartments and wondered whether Susan owned or rented hers. Unless her family had money, he did not think that a physiotherapist would be able to afford to buy here.

   He kept looking and thinking and knew that he was just putting off the moment of meeting with her. He finally made a move and was in the act of getting out of the car, when he saw her front door open. He saw a man exit the apartment and saw Susan standing at the door waving him goodbye. The man got into the car that was parked in the parking area across from Susan's. Henry's heart did a somersault in his chest and he got back into his car. He felt stricken and could not think what to do. 'Go home', his brain told him, and he started the car and drove carefully out of the compound and back to his house.

Once at home, he was annoyed with himself, that he did not go to Susan. The fact that he had seen a man leaving, meant nothing at all. It could have been a plumber or a relative. He hoped in his heart that Susan had not found someone else.

In the hospital next day, he went to the floor where her department was. She was in the office writing up notes when he knocked and entered. She looked surprised to see him but smiled warmly.

'Hi Susan, just wanted to say hello,' Henry said softly, 'I have missed you. You know?'

'I have been a bit preoccupied Henry the past couple of weeks. I have missed seeing you too.' Susan smiled, but Henry thought it looked like a sad smile.

Henry felt uplifted and said, 'What are you doing this coming weekend?'

Susan hesitated and said, 'Henry, please take this the right way. I need some time to sort a few things out. As soon as it's sorted, let's arrange a weekend away somewhere, anywhere, please.' She looked at him pleadingly.

Henry was startled by her reply. What did it mean?

'Susan, if there is someone else in your life, I will understand, believe me.'

Immediately she shook her head and said, 'No Henry, of course there isn't. It's something completely different that needs sorting.' She looked so serious and bit her lip.

He could see that she was on the verge of tears. He reached out and put his hand on her shoulder. 'Susan, if there is anything, I can do for you, you know where I am.' He left the office and went back to his own department.

Later that day he rang the hospital administrator and made an appointment to see her. He gave a lot of thought to the job situation and would have liked to discuss it with Susan but that seemed out of the question now. He would just try to be patient. Poor Susan, he hoped that whatever the problem was, that it would be sorted out satisfactorily. He wanted to take up where they had left off. His next call was to the university. He made an appointment with the professor of psychiatry there, the new man, and had a short chat about what he was hoping to do.

There now, it was done. All he could do was wait and see. Two part time jobs would be great, he thought. Time for family and time for researching if he was going to lecture students. Life could be challenging again. He needed a change after all the drama in his recent life.

Chapter 27

Marianne was a bit moody of late and Henry had been too involved with his own problems to really notice. He put it down to hormones. She wondered why Susan had not been around with her violin as she had promised. Henry told her that she had problems to sort out and no, he did not know what they were. He assured her that when all was well, a trip could be forthcoming. Mark overheard and immediately jumped in with, 'What about a trip to Disneyland, Dad?'

Henry thought that would be lovely, if rather expensive! On seeing his son's disappointed face, he said that they would have a big conversation soon with Susan as well. Jack's opinion would also have to be considered. That cheered Mark up. He knew that his Dad was being serious.

Marianne went on a bit about how cramped her bedroom was and why could she not move into the bedroom her mother had? Henry stopped what he was doing and looked at his daughter. She was quite a young lady now and filling out in all the right places. He looked at her with a smile and said, 'Why not indeed, and you would have your own bathroom.'

She looked at him to make sure that he meant it and then jumped up in the air and shouted 'Yes!'

The next afternoon, they decided on the big move. It was understood that Mark would now move into Marianne's bedroom, so he was excited as well. They went and surveyed what needed to be done. Everything was more-or-less as Marianne wanted it. She had a desk to be brought in and a bookshelf. They both lifted the emptied bookshelf into the bigger bedroom and then the desk, and of course all her old cuddly toys. The room had been decorated about five years ago and was quite pretty and fresh. Henry suggested that new bed linen would be nice, and Marianne agreed. The only thing out of place was the wardrobe, which was taking up too much space where it was. Henry thought it would be better placed on the shorter wall of the room. The two of them started to push and pull the empty wardrobe out from the wall to manoeuvre it across to the other wall. Mark was bringing Marianne's books in and putting them on the bed for her to arrange later. He saw his father pushing the big wardrobe and went to help them. It was moving but slowly. There seemed to be something sticking somewhere and Henry moved behind to see what it could be. There was something protruding from the back of the wardrobe down at floor level. Henry bent down to dislodge it, then stopped suddenly. He went down on his knees to see and felt a wave of nausea wash over him. It was a knife, a very long thin bladed one with a black handle protruding from the floor of the wardrobe. The back of the wardrobe had come away slightly from the base, allowing the knife to slip out. He rose slowly and stood looking down. The children had stopped pushing and came around to see what their father was looking at. They had asked him, but he had not answered. They were frightened when they saw his face.

'What is that Dad? Is it a knife?' Mark was curious and went down on his knees intending to pick it up.

'Don't, Mark! Leave it there! Don't touch it whatever you do.' Henry turned to Marianne.

'Come on, we have to leave that there for now. Come downstairs and we'll finish this later.'

The children knew better than to argue when their father used this tone of voice and they trooped slowly downstairs. Marianne was morose. When would the move take place now, she wondered?

He told the children to make some hot chocolate and have a break for a while. He went back upstairs to his office and slowly picked up his phone and rang the police station. He asked if Miller or Jones was available and got put through to Jones. After a short conversation, Henry went back downstairs to the children. They were sitting in silence in the kitchen eating biscuits that Ivy had made earlier in the week and drinking hot chocolate. They stared at their father in silence. Mark asked his father if that was the knife in the murder case? Henry did not know what to say. He never spoke of the murder in front of the children.

Now he realised, that they must have heard things spoken of, outside or in school. Children were naturally curious.

'I just don't know, Mark, I thought it better if I let the police take it, fingerprints and all that.'

Mark nodded his head solemnly and took another biscuit. Marianne stopped eating and stared at her father.

'Why is it in Mum's room, Dad? She didn't do it, did she?' Marianne looked distressed.

Henry breathed heavily. 'No Marianne, your poor mother certainly did not do it. I don't know why she would have put it there, maybe she found it and suspected it was the weapon, I just don't know.'

After thirty minutes, the doorbell rang. Mark ran out before Henry could get off his stool. Detective Jones entered and greeted them all. There was another man with him, not Miller.

Henry let the way up the stairs with a sinking heart. They went into the room and Jones pulled on gloves and went behind the wardrobe. He came out holding the knife, which looked rusty along the blade. They looked at it and then put it into a plastic bag, not before young Mark had a good look at it and said, 'Oh I've seen a knife like that before. I think it's a boning knife.'

Henry and Jones looked down at Mark and asked him where he had seen such a knife.

'Well it's got the same handle as the others, the ones in the block. You know those blocks that have a lot of knives stuck in them?'

The men nodded and with all the attention focused on Mark, he suddenly got shy and self-conscious. His face reddened and he suddenly bolted out the door of the bedroom and ran into his own bedroom. Henry looked in amazement at Jones and shook his head.

'I'll have a word with him later. He may just be excited and did not mean what he said and is now embarrassed.'

Jones nodded but said that he would also like a word with Mark. He thanked Henry for ringing him and said that this might be vital evidence. Henry said that he understood this.

'Whatever it shows up, I will never believe that my wife killed anybody, do you understand?'

Jones started walking down the stairs and said that they would keep him informed.

Marianne was weeping softly in the kitchen. To distract her, Henry said that they had work to do to get the room ready.

'Come on, young lady Let's get the show on the road. You want to be in by tonight, don't you?'

Marianne slowly got to her feet and they went silently up the stairs. Henry knocked at Mark's door in passing and said loudly, 'Out you come Mark, we need your help. We are not finished yet.'

Mark emerged from his room. He was silent and a little pale, Henry thought. He probably feels embarrassed and a bit of a fool, he thought, as he tousled the young boy's hair.

The rooms were sorted by seven o'clock and both were content. Marianne was very happy with her arrangement of the room and having her own bathroom was still quite unbelievable for her. No more waiting for Mark to vacate the bathroom in the morning! This is luxury, she thought.

Henry decided to send out for a takeaway as Ivy had not been there today. Most days now, she came in around midday and cleaned and ironed, the usual chores she always did. She also left a prepared dinner that they could either reheat in the microwave or if uncooked, put in the oven, with written instructions on how long to leave it in. Her daughter had recently started treatment for cancer and so her hours with the family were curtailed. She was always there when the children returned from school and then left soon after. Henry and she hoped that she would be able to resume her normal work hours in the future. In the meanwhile, she was a needed granny to three children, although they were now teenagers. Marianne and Mark missed her. She was like a granny to them.

After their Chinese dinner, they all sat and watched a video. Henry chose a lighthearted and funny one. He was aware of Mark's silence and knew that something was bothering him. He guessed that it the knife business. He decided that no mention of it would be made at all. If Mark was disturbed, he might approach him without feeling silly.

At ten o'clock Henry said, 'Bedtime, for us all. I'm tired after all that shifting of stuff. We might go and look for new bed linen tomorrow, right? Mark you need some new stuff too, that room you have now is a bit girly, I think.'

Mark nodded and added brightly, 'Can we paint the walls, Dad. Pink is not a boy's colour! I like the bed though, it's bigger than the one I had.'

So, it was arranged. Tomorrow was Saturday and everyone was free. There were no football matches, for a change. Henry would sit down and draft out a rough plan of what he wanted to discuss with both the hospital and university. He needed to plan how his proposed new job would work and what it would entail.

They picked up a tin of paint and brushes in Mark's chosen colour and then proceeded to the library. Marianne wanted to look for new books and Mark had books to renew. In the queue, Henry found himself beside the detective, Jones. He hardly recognised him outside the usual station and nodded to him. He had three boys with him. He drew near to Henry and said that the boys usually took ages to choose books and he always waited at the coffee bar beside the library. Would Henry consider dropping in casually so that he could ask Mark that question? Henry thought, why not? He nodded and waited in line. Mark renewed his books and Henry told Marianne to take her time, that he and Mark would go to the coffee bar. They headed over and were joined shortly by Jones. Mark looked a bit taken aback when the detective sat opposite them. Henry started a casual conversation about the football matches that weekend. Mark was busy with putting miniature marshmallows into his hot chocolate. Henry asked about the knife.

'Oh, there were only hundreds of those knives sold all over,' said Jones. 'They stopped making them about five years ago, but half the population of this town and many other towns would probably still have them in their house. They were used a lot for barbeques, seemingly.'

'That's where I saw it.' Mark nodded his head excitedly.

'Ah, yes, I'd say they were common enough,' said Jones off-handedly. 'I showed it to the others at the station, and about six people there had the same ones, so it's a difficult one, isn't it?'

It was Henry who eventually got the talk around to Mark and where he had seen it.

'Probably at Tommy's house, was it? I'd say they have quite a few barbeques in the summer with the gang they have, eh Mark?'

Just as Mark was about to reply, Marianne joined them and was excited about the book she had been looking for, for months.

'Why did you not just order it? That's what you should do,' said Mark, knowingly.'

Jones coughed and said, 'Well, all this talk of barbeques is making me hungry, I can't remember when we last had one. The boys love 'em.' He made pleading eye contact with Henry.

'We had one fairly recently, didn't we? With Susan and Jack, remember?' Henry looked down at Mark. 'It was a cracking one, if I do say so myself. Might have a look for those types of knives, we don't have anything good enough for the ribs, I think.'

Mark nodded. 'I just love ribs. That's where I saw the knife, Viv says it is a boning knife, for separating the ribs.'

Henry looked rather taken aback and looked at Jones who got to his feet and said he had to be going, or the boys would take up residence in the library.

Later that same afternoon, Jones and Miller had a meeting at the station with the boss and told them of their various findings. Things were knitting together gradually, and they felt the end was near.

Henry began painting Mark's bedroom after lunch. It gave him time to think about what Mark said. But in all probability those knives were very common as

Jones had remarked. Why was it in Lizzie's wardrobe, what made her put it there and where had she found it? He cursed himself for his stupidity, he had almost forgotten that she was in the house where Linda met her gruesome death. Why did she take it home, why not leave it there? Did she know the killer and was she protecting him or her and why? He would never be able to stop asking these questions and his brain felt bruised. Mark inspected his work regularly and approved of his choice of colour.

Chapter 28

Doctor Kumar was an Indian gynaecologist in her late forties. She had been working in Belgium for the past twenty years. Her brother who was murdered was seven years younger than her and they had both trained in the same hospital. When he died, she had been working in London. Her brother was very ambitious, she told detective Miller and very bright. He had a brilliant future ahead of him she thought.

She did not see that much of him as he was a junior doctor and working all hours and she was a senior registrar, also working long hours. They kept in touch by Skype and emails. She thought that he was involved romantically, with a young doctor for a while. But suddenly he was very excited about the attention that a professor was showing him. He was flattered by it and knew that this professor could see what a brilliant mind he had, that's the story she was told. She had not realised that there was a sexual element to the relationship at first. When it became clear, she said that she was shocked. She warned her brother that for a tutor or lecturer to start such a relationship was all wrong and would end badly. She felt that her brother was being manipulated for whatever reason by this woman, who was years older than her brother.

For a while, she stopped communicating with him. Her family in India started asking her for information about his progress, as he was not good at getting in touch with them. Eventually, she contacted him again. He was working very hard and was still seeing the professor. He explained that he did not see her all the time, as she was a lecturer in various other hospitals.

The next information she had, was a police message for her to get in touch with them as soon as possible. She and her family were devastated by the murder of such a young and promising doctor. She had attended the inquest alone. The verdict was unlawful killing by person or persons unknown. It was still an open case and she and the family would dearly love to get closure. She had, herself, asked questions at the hospital about the whereabouts of his girlfriend but learned nothing. Nobody seemed to be aware of his relationship with Professor Smythe. She was left wondering whether it was a figment of his imagination! Then she spoke to an older consultant and when she mentioned Smythe's name, she felt an immediate withdrawal of the man. He was suddenly very brusque and said he was very busy and really knew nothing about her brother and any woman. A matron at the same hospital understood that a young attractive doctor had been very infatuated with her brother and thought that there was a real romance there, but it seemed to come to an end when the young lady moved away to another position.

She never got to meet the professor who did not attend the inquest and she never received any note of sympathy or condolence.

Miller relayed all this to Jones and the boss. Interesting as it was, they could not tie the case up with the murder of the professor. The boss asked about the girlfriend. Did anyone know who she was and where she was now? Miller explained that the hospital records department was going to send him up a list of doctors who were working in the same hospital as Kumar, but it would take time. There was also no guarantee that the woman worked in the same hospital as he did.
All they could hope for, was that a name would jump out at them that they recognised.

Jones related his news, which took some time. Eventually, the boss said, 'I think we should bring her in as soon as possible, don't you?' Jones agreed and went outside to make a phone call.

Susan was bringing Jack to the sports hall for physical training when she got the message. She asked a friend at the hall if she would bring Jack home to her mother's house, if she was delayed. There was something she must attend to.

She drove straight away to the police station and knew where to go. She had been there a couple of times before. She liked detective Jones. He was a father and had children and was very sympathetic.

Today there were two other men in the room, which was unusual. She took a seat beside Jones and opposite the other two men. She was introduced and nodded.

At once the boss asked her if she had kept to the instructions that they had given her?

'Yes, of course. I have not been out with Doctor Dukes since detective Jones spoke to me.'

'Have you had any more silent phone calls?' Miller asked her.

'I have had about five silent calls late at night, and the other six had a sort of distorted, disembodied voice, somewhat threatening and sinister. I cannot tell whether the voice is male or female. I was warned about my son being in danger from Doctor Dukes, that he was a pervert. The next calls warned me that he had murdered his wife and that I was in danger.'

'Did the caller's number show up on any of these calls? Or did you hear any other background sounds at all, to give you a clue as to the whereabouts of this caller?' Jones asked this hopefully, although he knew it was probably futile.

Susan nodded. 'The last call made, a couple of nights ago, I'm sure I could hear Henry – Doctor

Dukes' voice in the background. He was explaining something medical, or using medical language, then there were glasses clinking, and then the call ended.'

Detective Miller asked her which night the call was made and what time?

They spoke for some length and considered putting a tap on her landline at home. She had received calls on both her landline and mobile. It was somebody who knew her and had access to her personal details.

When Susan had left, the men discussed the situation again and were certain that they were on the right track. The fingerprints found at the murdered Kumar's flat, matched the ones in the professor's basement flat. This was the murderer, they knew. The only common denominator was Henry Dukes. Susan Dillon had never met Linda Smythe, or Doctor Kumar and as far as they knew, Henry Dukes had never met Doctor Kumar.

By the end of the week the list arrived from the south and Jones got a list of tenants of Linda's basement apartment. The two got together on Friday afternoon to study both lists in the hope of finding a common name.

Chapter 29

Henry spent Thursday speaking with the hospital administrator in the morning and the Dean of Studies at the university in the afternoon. Both interviews went well. The hospital administrator had no problem with job sharing. She thought that it would be very common in the future and so long as his hours were arranged and agreed upon, a contract could be drawn up and pension adjusted, and all the legalities attended to. The man at the university told Henry what it was that they expected and asked Henry how he planned to organise his hours. There were a certain number of hours expected and after discussing it, they both thought that it was feasible.

Henry drove home very happy with the progress and was quite excited about the change. He would have more time free and if he wanted to continue some private clinical work he could. He did not think that he would be out of pocket at all, or if he was, it would not be by very much.

He settled down after dinner with the children, to read the contract offered by the university and study the small print. He was greatly surprised when his phone rang and a familiar voice said, 'Hi Henry, how are you, it's been so long'.

It was Susan and Henry's heart skipped a beat. 'Susan! What a lovely surprise, and one I was not expecting.'

It was a long phone call and Henry was thrilled. He told her about the change of job at the beginning of the call and Susan thought that a change would be a good thing for him. They discussed what was involved and she said that the children would benefit from having their father around more. Then she gave him her news. It was rather mysterious to Henry. She said that the business that she had to settle would soon be settled and that she would be able to see him again and explain all. Then she asked, 'What about a super holiday for us all? I'm thinking Disneyland in Paris. I know it is expensive, and I will of course be paying for myself and Jack, but what do you think of the idea Henry?'

Henry could only laugh. He told her about Mark asking the same question a while back and mentioning the same destination. He was amazed by the coincidence.

'I guess it's fate. I know the children will love it and we will enjoy it too, I hope. I think it's a great idea, Susan. Can I tell Mark and Marianne soon, they will be so excited and it's something to look forward to, isn't it?'

'Henry, we'll tell them and Jack in two weeks' time, alright? On our next outing together.'

Henry asked her how she was keeping and how was Jack? They were away for a week, just the two of them. He asked her where and she laughed and said, 'You'll never guess in a million years – Barra in the Outer Hebrides!' Henry asked her if she was joking and was told no, she had relatives there and was paying a long overdue visit.

Henry sat on the sofa and sighed contentedly. Life was settling at last; the girl still liked him, or did she love him? No, that was too strong a word, wasn't it? She probably loved him, he thought. No, that was wrong, *possibly* loved him, would that be right? He gave up and went upstairs to tell the children that it was bedtime. He looked so happy that his daughter immediately guessed something had happened.

'What are you so happy about, Dad? You look as though you have found a box of treasure!'

'Ah, that would be telling you now. In two weeks, I might have some interesting news for the two of you.' On being begged to tell them, he just shook his head and said they must be patient.

He told his colleagues at work the next day about his change of job. They were intrigued and thought it a sound idea. Henry was known as a great lecturer and tutor and they thought it would be a job that he would enjoy immensely.

About three o'clock he got a distressed phone call from his sister, Betts. Their mother, Iris, was in hospital since midday, with a suspected stroke. She was at the hospital with a friend of her mother's and asked if he could come immediately. Of course, Henry said he was leaving straight away.

He told his manager and was told to take whatever time was needed. He went home to pack a few things and spoke with Ivy. She said that she would be there for the children when they returned from school, unfortunately she could not stay the night. Henry thought for a moment, and then realised that Susan was away too. Ivy suggested that perhaps Dr. Viv could come and stay with the two. He nodded and said, 'Of course, I'll ring her now.'

He got on to Viv and she said that she would be delighted to come and stay with the children

'I hate putting you out Viv, if you want them to stay at your place it's fine with me. It's taking advantage of you, I know.'

'You know that I love being with the children, Henry and no, I think it's better for them to stay in their own home and keep to their usual routine.

It was arranged. She would come over after work and let Ivy go to her daughter's. The weekend was coming up and there would be plenty to do with the children.

Henry promised that he would keep her posted about his mother. There was no point bringing the children up at this stage and hopefully the news would be good, and they could visit their grandmother later when she was recuperating.

Henry left with a lighter heart and told Ivy that he would ring the children as soon as he got to the hospital and talk to them. As he drove, he could not help thinking about the last emergency dash he made for his father. He hoped that his mother would not be seriously incapacitated and that it was just a minor stroke. It did not seem so long since his father had died. He sighed and thought how a phone call can change everything. The good news of the past twenty-four hours diminished suddenly, and he wondered if this was his life now, up in the air one moment, only to be dashed down again, the next.

The hospital seemed quiet compared to the hospital he worked in. He found Betts with an older woman, a friend of Iris. Betts ran to him and hugged him. He could see that she was stressed and knew that she could not handle stress well. Her personality depended on life around her being tranquil and orderly. When he saw his mother, he was shocked. When had she aged so? He knew that she was elderly, but the woman in the bed looked so shrunken and grey and so old. Had he never looked properly at his mother before? He had expected to find her as elegant as ever, composed, always smiling and in charge of everything. He was told by a nurse that the doctor would speak to him later. They were expecting him. Betts relied on Henry to explain all that was happening.

Of course, there was no real news as such, the woman had suffered a stroke, they thought. It was too early to say how bad it might be. Tomorrow they could do tests and hope that she would regain consciousness.

They went wearily home. Henry rang the children and told them what he could. Then he spoke to Viv. They both knew that it was a waiting game. He also rang Grace and told her the news. She wanted to help of course and was free to go to the children. Henry asked if that would be possible as Viv had to work, and he did not know how long he would be needed. Grace said that she would make arrangement at home. Millie and Anne were always on hand to help. Her four children were of an age where they could look after themselves and John would be looked after by them all. He was rather spoilt and hated having to change his routine. She thought that it would do him good to have to adapt. It was now late so he would ring Viv tomorrow and let her know that Grace was coming.

The children were happy to have Viv stay with them as they liked her a lot. They sat eating popcorn for an hour before bedtime and chatted. Viv asked them what they would like to do over the weekend, and they thought about that. They eventually both agreed on a visit to the zoo on Saturday. Maybe a movie on Sunday? They chatted happily. Marianne told Viv that her Dad had good news before Granny Iris became ill.

'We have to wait for two weeks before we know what this exciting news is', she explained, 'but Dad was very happy looking, wasn't he Mark?'

Mark agreed with her. 'I think he might have decided on that holiday I suggested, Disneyland, wouldn't that be great? We will have to discuss it with Susan and Jack of course first. Imagine us all going to Paris, wouldn't that be cool?'

Marianne put on her pouting face. 'We have not seen Susan for ages, and she promised to bring over her violin and play duets with me. I wish she would tell me when she is coming over.'

'Maybe she is busy with work too. Physiotherapy is a busy job, you know,' explained Viv.'

'I'm sure Jack is dying to come over, I gave him some Lego and he was so happy. He can make amazing things and so fast, you would not believe it!' Mark nodded his head vigorously.

Later when upstairs getting ready for bed, Mark showed Viv his newly painted room. She admired it and thought that it was a perfect boy's room and that his Dad did a great job painting it.

Marianne showed Viv her new bedroom with pride and her own bathroom. 'We got new bed linen too.'

'Guess what we found behind the wardrobe, Viv,' interrupted Mark. 'A knife, would you believe, just like one of your boning knives.'

Viv laughed and said, 'That's a funny place for a knife, Mark. What did you do with it?'

Marianne said seriously, 'Dad phoned the police immediately and would not let us even touch it. They came and took it away with them.'

'Really?' Viv was surprised. 'Why was it in the wardrobe, I wonder? I suppose it could have been there for a long time.'

'I hope it was not the one that killed that lady professor. Tommy told me about that murder. Right on our own doorstep, he said.'

Henry rang Viv that night to tell her about Grace coming down. He was not sure when exactly she would arrive but had told Grace to ring Viv and let her know.

'Henry, there was really no need to get poor Grace to come down, you know. We will manage fine. I am here to get the children off to school and then I'll go to work. Ivy will be there when they return.'

'Viv, I know very well that you will cope. However, Ivy has had problems with her daughter recently and must spend a lot of her free time over there with her and her grandchildren. Anyway, hopefully I will be home in a few days. There will be tests and scans to be done on my mother first.'

'Alright Henry, no worries. Everything here is fine and the children and I are off to the zoo tomorrow and the movies on Sunday. They are great planners!'

'Viv just don't let them take advantage of your good nature. I think they can twist you round their little fingers! Make them do their chores too, don't spoil the little monkeys!'

'Not at all Henry, they spoil me, they are so loving and good. I'm mad about them,' she laughed.

The weekend was spent pleasantly with a trip to the zoo. Mark recalled the snake story for Viv. They walked for a long time and by five o'clock the three were tired. They got a Chinese takeaway and went home to eat it and relax in front of the television.

Chapter 30

Detectives Miller and Jones had been crouched over their desks all day, comparing their lists and checking notes. Apart from the boss popping his head around the door several times already, they were silent in their searches.

'Have one here, mate, a Doctor Don O'Sullivan, worked with Kumar, attended lectures of Smythe.'

Miller scratched his chin and searched through another list, turning over pages in a frustrated manner. 'I'm sure I came across that name before,' he murmured.

Jones ran his index finger down a list of names on his list. 'Have you come across a John Mardy?'

Miller said no. After more page shifting, he said, 'Yes, gotcha! He read from his notes, 'Don O'Sullivan, flatmate of Doctor Kumar. Oh dear! No good! Committed suicide. I guess we can cross him off.'

'When did he top himself, before or after Kumar?' Jones looked up at Miller.

'Looks like he did it about six months before Kumar died. So, he didn't kill Kumar.'

'They do have Smythe in common though, don't they?' Miller asked.

'If we are just listing everyone who had a link with her, we'll run out of paper.' Jones laughed and threw his pencil down. 'It's Friday night, lad, we should be down the pub with the lads instead of being up here, chasing our tails.'

'One more hour and then we're out of here,' Miller said. 'The boss will have us in here over the weekend otherwise and my missus will go mad.'

They worked again in silence and the sound of rolled up balls of paper hitting the wastepaper basket was the only sound. Then there was a low whistle from Jones.

He pushed his paper across the desk and told Miller to have a look. When Miller looked, he raised his eyebrows and shrugged.

'It could be something and it could be nothing. Lots of people stayed at that basement flat over the years, but it is worth investigating, I think.'

Jones suggested that Miller check that name against his list from down south. The hospital list from Kumar's hospital was almost all checked, and nothing matched the name that Jones found. He pulled out the next hospital in the area and started looking. 'Wouldn't you think that all these lists would be computerised?' He grumbled to himself, scratching his head with his pencil.

Then he stopped and checked again, then went to his notes. Looking up he said slowly, 'Jonesy boy, I think we may have hit the jackpot.'

Jones went over to see and whistled again. 'Now we have the same person in the same places, but do we have a murderer?'

Miller was already reaching for his phone. 'We have to find the connection with Kumar, don't we? That will be first. If we can establish that, we start digging here and hopefully will strike it rich.'

Over the next couple of days, Miller reached Dr. Kumar, finally and put his request to her. Seeing as she had trained in the same hospital as her brother, she surely had some old acquaintances she could contact for the information they were seeking? She was very helpful and promised that she would look up anyone she knew from her days there. She was also very anxious to find her brother's murderer.

On Monday, Henry spoke with the consultant treating his mother. The scan showed a small bleed on the right side of the brain. Right now, it did not seem to be still bleeding and there was no loss of movement. She was a little confused however, and they thought that if there was no further deterioration that she could be discharged in a week.

On Tuesday when Henry went into the hospital, Iris was sitting up in bed. She smiled when she saw him and said, 'Henry, I'm so glad to see you, am I going to be alright?'

He was amazed at her lucidity. 'Mum, how are you feeling, and do you know what happened?'

'I imagine that I've had a turn or stroke, though I can move my limbs.' Iris smiled wryly, 'Poor Betts must have got a fright.'

'Mum, can you remember what you were doing on Thursday last and how you were feeling?'

'Of course, I can remember. I was in the garden picking up branches and debris. I had been pruning the shrubs earlier. I was busy bending down a lot to gather the stuff up and then putting them in the wheelbarrow. I must have spent the best part of the morning doing that. After my coffee at twelve, I got dizzy and felt a headache coming on. After that, it's a bit confused.'

Henry felt quite relieved. His mother was lucid and remembered what she had been doing. He thought it was a turn due to lack of oxygen to the brain, with all the bending down and then straightening up. He knew his mother's energy in the garden, she had always looked after the garden and it was a considerable size. He would have a word with her doctor and give him the details. A rest in hospital for a few days would not do her any harm, he thought.

Grace had rung Henry and Viv to apologise and said that due to unforeseen circumstances, she would not be able to come down until Thursday at the earliest. Viv told her that it was not a problem at all. By Tuesday, Henry rang Grace and told her that the crisis was over, his mother was being discharged and was in good form again. He would be returning home on Thursday, after seeing his mother settled back in. She was already complaining about the fuss. He was relieved and delighted to see Iris back to her old self and Betts happy again.

He drove back on Thursday evening and was quite exhausted when he stepped into his hall. Viv and the children were waiting for him. Having regaled them with news about Granny Iris, they departed to bed satisfied. He was starving and was grateful for the hot dinner that awaited him. Viv sat and told him all about their exploits since he was away. Mark had scored a goal at the match on Monday night. Marianne had her music lesson and was progressing very well. They went into the sitting room and watched the news. Viv got Henry a whisky and she had a glass of wine. He told her the news about the job sharing. She was surprised and asked him if he was sure this was what he wanted. They discussed various ways of looking at it. Viv knew that Henry was excited about this and said it was just what was needed to perk him up. He felt revived just speaking about the job and outlined what he hoped to do. He thought he had the best of both worlds. They discussed the Health department's view of the overall planning for the county and they were of the same mind. Henry yawned and Viv got up and took his glass. He got up to turn off the television. She returned with both glasses replenished and he sat down again. After a while he found himself nodding off but could hear Viv talking about the children. He made the effort to pay more attention. When he had finished his drink, he could no longer keep his eyes open and apologised to Viv. She laughed and told him he would sleep well and that he should take it easy this weekend after all the worry. Then she remembered that she had a form for him to sign. Would he mind being a referee for the sale of her uncle's house, something the banks required until they had the deeds. Henry hardly heard her but saw her produce the form and a pen. He leaned on the table and signed his name. She told him that she would be in touch later in the week and to ring her if he needed anything. She left and he stumbled up to bed, asleep before his head touched the pillow.

Chapter 31

Henry felt washed out the next morning and was glad to see Ivy in early. She was interested to hear how his mother was and happy that he was home again. He said that he had drunk too much whisky the night before and was a bit hungover. Ivy laughed and said it was understandable after the week he had spent up with his mother, not knowing if she was going to make it. He enquired about Ivy's daughter and sympathised with the woman when he heard that some of the scans were ambiguous. It seemed that chemotherapy would be started soon, and Henry offered to help in any way he could. He also told Ivy that she must organise her hours with his family to suit her own needs. The children were growing up fast and were quite capable of doing chores around the house.

When he went to his office and reacquainted himself with his clinical duties that week, he first rang home to check on his mother. Betts answered and said that her mother was fine and wanted to go gardening again. One of her friends was staying over for a while and would keep an eye on her while she worked at the school catering, which was only for a few hours most days.

Susan rang that evening before Henry left the office and sounded a bit strained. He immediately asked her if all was well with her and Jack. Susan said all was well, but she would have to wait another week or so before they could meet up. She apologised and said she was feeling a bit frustrated about all the delay and cloak and dagger stuff. Henry laughed and said that he was fascinated by it and could hardly wait to hear what it was all about.

'So long as you are still talking to me and looking forward to that holiday, I can wait patiently,' he told her.

'Henry, I am so looking forward to being with you and the children again and Jack has been pestering me about visiting Mark. It's hard on the child. I'm running out of excuses.'

At the police station, the two men were still poring over lists of names. There were a few names on them that could not be contacted, whether they had emigrated, died, or left medicine was difficult to ascertain. Then the lab at that moment, faxed through their analysis of the knife found in the Dukes' house.

'Well, well, look at this, Jonesy. Fingerprints were those of Lizzie Dukes and the blood was certainly that of the Smythe woman, but under the hilt, which was a bit dented, they found traces of blood from Doctor Kumar.'

'I can't believe they can identify traces that old,' protested Jones. 'Is it true?'

'That's what the analysis form states, and I believe in this science, Jones.'

'I think it a bit silly that the same knife was used twice. Arrogant, don't you think? I wonder what a psychologist would make of that?' Jones looked over at his partner with raised eyebrows.

'Well, Lizzie was never in that part of the country and was a lot younger than Kumar, so there is definitely a second killer. Perhaps the weapon was so successful the first time, the killer had an attachment to it.' Miller grinned at his friend.

An hour later an email came through which made the two men very hopeful. It was from Doctor Kumar in Belgium. She was on her way over to her former hospital, where she had done her training and was going to see a few people who were still around from that time. She hoped to speak to Don O'Sullivan's mother and sister. She would be in touch with them.

When the boss called in to see how things were progressing, they were able to put a smile on his large face.

Chapter 32

Mrs. O'Sullivan lived with her unmarried daughter who was a nurse. She had been heartbroken when her son took his own life. She was happy to talk to Doctor Kumar about him. Her daughter told the Indian doctor that she loved to talk about Don and was happier afterwards. So many people refused to talk to her about it, maybe because they thought it would upset the woman, but the opposite was true. Yes, some tears would be shed, but later she would be much calmer and happy.

Dr. Kumar had tea with both women. She explained why she had started to research her brother's murder after so long. Her own mother had died, not knowing who her son's killer was and she had, herself, given up on the case ever being solved until recently. Now she was going to do all she could to help the police close the case.

She thought that she would start with Don's mother as he and her brother were flatmates. She mentioned how strange it was, that both should die within six months of each other.

She read the letter that Don had left for his mother. It was a sad emotional one. Don had been a hard worker and achieved a First Class Honours degree. He told his mother that he had loved everything about medicine and thanked her for the sacrifices she and his father had made for him to do medicine. He wrote how sorry he was for letting her down. He could not continue with his life, it was unbearable. He knew he was depressed and despised himself for giving up. His heart was broken, and he had no desire to go on living. He would never be able to help anyone as he was so injured himself. His troubles had been based on pride. He thought that he was so intelligent and had been told so by a woman he had admired so much. She had loved him, and he was so flattered that he had thought that he loved her. Indeed, he had loved her.

Then he discovered that his flatmate was having an affair with her and was distraught, especially as *his* girlfriend was so lovely and he knew that she was pregnant. He had talked to his friend and pleaded with him not to get involved with this woman. His friend thought that he was only jealous and laughed at him. His girlfriend came to Don and asked if he would warn Kumar off the woman who was also his tutor. The girl was desperate and three months pregnant and in love with Kumar. Confronted by the two of them, Kumar confessed to being obsessed with his tutor and believed that he had a future with her, despite both Don and Kumar's girlfriend's pleading. At this stage, Don knew that Kumar had also been taken in by their tutor. In the end, Don was forsaken by Kumar, his friend and the manipulative tutor.

When Doctor Kumar had finished the letter, she put it on the table in front of the mother. She wiped her eyes and said she was sorry and thanked her for sharing the story with her. Now she knew the truth and how her brother had betrayed his friend and girlfriend. But did he deserve to be killed because of it, or was he killed for another reason, a different reason and by whom? They did not know the name of the girlfriend. Don's sister thought that she might be able to find out as a friend was married to a doctor who may have known her. Doctor Kumar hoped that she would be able to do that, as soon as possible.

Miller got a phone call the next morning telling him of the progress made. A story was beginning to emerge, and he was sure it would answer a lot of questions. He was of the opinion himself, that there was another male involved with Smythe at the same time as Kumar and that this had led to a crime of passion. Therefore, he put a lot of work into investigating the other males who had worked with Kumar. One man had already committed suicide over his infatuation with Smythe, how many others were there. He found himself going into a reverie, wondering just what sort of woman had she been, to have this power over men?

Chapter 33

Henry was busy in the coming weeks, reorganising his work schedules and getting ready to start lectures at the university. He was both nervous and excited. He felt rejuvenated and had a spring in his step that had been missing for some time. Marianne noticed him humming away as he worked in the kitchen after dinner. She immediately thought of Susan.

'Hey Dad, when are we getting this good news? Have you forgotten all about it?

'Indeed, I have not, and it should be very soon now, my pet.'

Mark, overhearing said loudly, 'I still think we all need a very BIG holiday. If you change jobs, you will be very busy, and you won't have time for holidays.'

'Mark and Marianne, I give you my word, we are going to have a holiday and it will be with Susan and Jack. It's still a secret where we are going, okay?'

The two children looked at each other in delight. 'Are we really all going together, Dad?'

Henry looked at them and put his finger to his lips. 'I have probably given away too much already. It was supposed to be a big secret.' He smiled at them and told them to keep it quiet until it was all arranged.

Ivy was absent for the week, taking care of her daughter and children. Henry drew up a roster of the jobs that needed doing each day and the three divided them up between them. Viv called around to see if they were all well and if she could do anything to help. She knew Ivy's daughter was in hospital and had visited her. She offered to take Marianne to her music as they were having a very wet spell just then. Mark's football training was cancelled for the week, but he had indoor athletics training. Henry had a clinic that night, so was grateful for Viv's involvement. When Viv arrived back at the house with the two, Henry was just arriving home. They all went into the warm sitting room. Viv made the children hot chocolate and had brought some homemade cookies. She made Henry a hot toddy with lemon and cloves, to keep the cold out, she said. She had a glass of red wine. As they sat enjoying their drinks, Mark piped up that they were all going on holiday soon. Viv raised her eyebrows and asked where they were going? Mark smiled and rushed on, 'Yes we are going away with Susan and Jack on a big holiday, very soon, aren't we Dad?'

Henry was a bit embarrassed. Nothing was definite yet, he explained, and it was to be a surprise. He looked at Mark and raised his eyebrows.

'Oh, sorry Dad! I forgot to keep it quiet! I'm a blabber-mouth, aren't I?' Anyway, it's only Viv and she is really family, isn't she?'

Viv laughed and said that he need not worry, she would not tell anyone, she was able to keep a secret.

Henry asked Mark for his sports bag so that he could put his sportswear into the wash to have ready for Saturday's match. He told the children it was bedtime and they put their cups into the kitchen and said goodnight to Viv. She took the glasses out to the kitchen. When Henry came from the utility room, he found Viv looking at the evening news and his whisky glass refilled. He laughed at her and said he hoped he would not be hungover like the last time. Viv smiled and told him it was only because he was so tired from driving from his mother's.

They spoke about Iris and how she was progressing and about Ivy and her sick daughter. Then Viv asked, 'Henry, are you serious about Susan?'

Henry felt himself blushing like a schoolboy and said quietly, 'Well, I think I am. She is a lovely person and we get along very well as do the children.'

Viv told him that she was glad he had found somebody and thought that they were well matched. 'You are lucky Henry, to find love twice in your life, some people don't even find it once.'

'I did not expect to, Viv, it just happened. She just appeared, at the right moment, I think. She has also had disappointment in her life, and her life revolves around Jack, being mildly autistic. I feel it will be a good partnership.' He finished his drink and excused himself to go up and say goodnight to the children.

When he came down again, his drink was again replenished and he remonstrated, laughing. 'Viv, I don't usually drink this amount of whisky, you know.'

'I know Henry, call it an early celebration of your future; your change of job, your relationship with Susan.' She raised her glass and said, 'To the future, Henry.'

She said she would see him during the week and if he needed a babysitter or a chauffeur, she was available.

Henry later awoke. He was still in the sitting room in his armchair. He felt very disoriented and dizzy. 'Bloody whisky,' he grumbled. He made himself get up and had trouble standing. He made his way to the kitchen unsteadily and made himself drink a pint of water. Then he climbed the stairs holding onto the banisters. He hadn't the energy to remove his clothes before falling into his bed.

The children ran into his room to wake him the following morning. 'Dad, your alarm did not go off. It's half eight and we're going to be late for school.' Marianne was upset. Mark was not too perturbed, being late to school would not be a problem for him.

Chapter 34

Henry was not feeling the best when he got a phone call at eleven o'clock that morning. He hated rushing and this morning's rush made him feel ill. It was the police and Henry groaned as he listened. They needed to see him as soon as possible. He said he would go to the station at lunch time if that would suit. The thoughts of food made him want to gag so he decided that missing the meal would be good.

He drove slowly down to the station, thinking that he was not really in a fit state to drive and hadn't been earlier either. He hoped no policeman would stop and breathalyse him.

The usual two were in the interview room that he was shown to. He sat down heavily.
Jones looked at him quickly and asked, 'Are you alright Doctor Dukes?'

Henry nodded and it seemed as if his head was ready to burst.

Miller explained that they were worried about his relationship with Susan as she had been receiving strange phone calls since she started going out with him. They had suggested that she stop seeing him for the moment while they investigated the phone calls. It was for her safety and that of her son, they said.

Henry did his best to look focused and said nothing.

Miller said that allegations had been made about her child not being safe in Henry's company, also that he was a suspect in his wife's murder. He stopped speaking and looked at Henry.

Jones looked at Henry and asked, 'Any thoughts on this matter, doctor?'

Henry said nothing and was having trouble absorbing what the two men were saying.

Jones sighed and went on, 'The knife found in your house had two samples of blood on it, the murdered professor and another murdered doctor in the south. He was murdered some eighteen years ago.'

Miller looked up from his notes and said, 'Doctor, your wife was never near the hospital where the other doctor worked, and we know that she did not kill him. That was someone else. Her fingerprints were on the knife so it's obvious that she took this knife from the crime scene to her home.'

Their voices were now sounding like hollow echoes to Henry and he seemed to be seeing them from a distance. Then their faces became enlarged and they loomed up, closer and closer to Henry, who put up his hands to keep them back. He tried to get to his feet but stumbled backwards and then he knew that he was falling, falling.

Susan got a phone call from Jones later that afternoon. He explained that Doctor Dukes had been admitted to hospital with an undisclosed illness. It was serious.

She went to the hospital straight away and spoke to the doctors who explained that they were doing tests but could not say what the doctor was suffering from right now. She was alarmed, especially when she saw a policeman outside his room. Was he being guarded, she wanted to know? They would not tell her, but she guessed he was. She rang her mother to keep Jack until she returned home. Then she contacted Jones and asked to see him.

At the station she was shown into a room with the two men she was acquainted with and a woman she never saw before. She was introduced to Doctor Kumar. She was anxious to hear about Henry and what they thought might be wrong with him. She wondered if his mother had been notified and hoped not, as she was recovering from a slight stroke, she thought. What about the children, she asked? Who was taking care of them?

She was told that the school had been notified when Henry was admitted to hospital at one thirty and that a neighbour would collect them from school.

Susan wondered who Doctor Kumar was and why she was in the room with them. When Miller asked her how she got on with her investigation of her brother's murder, she started to speak.

Chapter 35

Susan went into the hospital again to see Henry. He was still unconscious and was in the Intensive Care Unit. She went to Kate's house, as she had met her before, and Jones said the children would be there. When Kate answered the door, she was surprised to see Susan. On asking about Henry, she was shocked to hear about his condition. No, the children were not with her, as Viv had called and told her she would be looking after them in their own house.

Susan called to see the children. Viv admitted her and asked if she had seen Henry recently? Susan reiterated what she had told Kate; he was still unconscious, and they still had not identified the illness. The children were subdued, and Mark was tearful, Marianne trying to put on a brave face. She went to Susan and Susan put her arms around her and told her that her Dad was strong and would be alright. Mark started crying softly.

Susan asked Viv if she wanted her to come and mind the children. She could bring Jack over and that might distract the older two. Viv shook her head.

'Susan, Henry was afraid of something like this happening a while ago and he gave me guardianship of the children. He always knew how much I loved them and how they like me.'

Susan was astounded. She never knew that and told Viv so. Viv asked her if she would help with their care and maybe mind them when she was busy with work?

'Of course, I will, Viv,' she mumbled, shocked at how things were progressing.

Later in the evening Susan rang Jones, whose mobile number she had and gave him the news. He was silent for a long time and then told Susan to go home and have a good night's sleep. He would be in touch.

Susan went home and was staying the night with her mum as Jack was already in bed. She rang Grace and gave her the news about Henry. She had not been notified about Henry and was shocked. She then told Grace about Viv being made guardian of the children and Grace told her that she did not believe that for a moment.

'Why would Henry do that,' she asked? 'We are their nearest relatives and surely, he would have discussed that with me?' Not that she had anything against Viv, she liked the woman, it was just such a drastic position to take and why? He was always so healthy!

Susan had no answer but was very perturbed, especially as she had heard what Doctor Kumar reported. She was not at liberty to divulge that information at present, so she said nothing. Grace was going to travel down the next day to see her brother-in-law. Susan was relieved to hear that.

At eleven o'clock that night, she drove back to the hospital to see how Henry was doing. She was weak with relief to hear that he was now conscious and responding to his surroundings. Jones and Miller had been to see him too. The police guard was still outside his room and the nurse told her that only she would be allowed in. She left the hospital feeling more optimistic.

After dropping Jack, the next morning, she went straight to the hospital to enquire about Henry. She was allowed enter the room and speak to him briefly. He was very groggy, and his speech was very slurred. She hoped that he had not got a brain injury. Her heart jumped in her chest when he looked at her and smiled. He knew her! She patted his hand and whispered, 'Get better soon, my darling.'

He gave her a lop-sided grin and tried to raise his hand. She left the room and wiped the tears from her cheeks.

When Grace arrived, she went straight to the hospital. Susan was there too. Before they went to see Henry, the doctor treating him arrived and they spoke with him. He was treating Henry for liver damage. He had taken a large amount of a chemical that could have been lethal. It would have been, except that his liver was healthy. If he was a serious drinker, he would have been dead by now. They were trying to flush out all the toxins that were in his system and they knew that he would survive. He just needed lots of rest.

The women went into the private room and saw that Henry was sleeping. They went outside and had a coffee. Grace was in shock and wanted to know what happened to put him in hospital. Susan shook her head. She did not know.

Chapter 36

When Grace called to the house later, she found Ivy in the utility room ironing. She told Ivy that Henry would survive, and all would be well. The woman was so relieved that she started to cry silently. She told Grace that a policeman had already been to the house to see if there was a bottle of alcohol or an empty bottle around. Although she had looked everywhere, even searched the dustbins, nothing was found. There was no medication or drugs of any description found either.

The children came home from school as usual and were overjoyed to find Grace there.
Was she alone or were her cousins there too? Grace explained that her twins were at school and busy studying for their exams and the other two were at college. She promised that they would all get together as soon as their dad was out of hospital. Mark thought that their big holiday with Susan and Jack would not now take place. Grace assured him that everything that his dad had planned would go ahead just as soon as he was up and about.

Viv arrived at six. Ivy had made the dinner and was ready to leave to go home. Viv was surprised to see Grace but welcomed her warmly. After dinner, the children were upstairs finishing their homework and the women were sitting in front of the television.

Grace told Viv that she had been allowed to visit Henry and the doctor told her that he would recover and had been extremely fortunate. Viv nodded and said that was wonderful news indeed. She admitted the children had been very fearful, especially after losing their mother so early in life.

Grace mentioned nothing about the guardianship that Susan had told her about. She declined a glass of wine and said that she was very tired.

'Viv, I will be here for as long as it takes Henry to recover and return home, so really, there is no need to put yourself out further. You have your job to go to in the morning and I'm sure you are missing being in your own home. You'll be able to visit him yourself very soon I imagine.'

Viv agreed that she missed her own space and had things to do at home. 'If you need me at any time to come over, just let me know, Grace. I will always be free for the children.'

A week later, Henry was now out of danger. Susan was sitting with Henry, when Miller and Jones came in. They had checked first with the hospital to make sure the patient was able for the visit. They found Henry sitting up in bed and looking happy, if pale.

They started to talk to Henry and all he needed to do was to listen. At some stage, Jones asked him if he was finding it too distressing to go on? Henry shook his head but reached for Susan's hand, holding it tightly.

They told him about the murder of Doctor Kumar and how his sister had travelled over from Belgium to assist them. She had been invaluable in her research. Through her they had been able to talk with a doctor who had performed an abortion on her brother's fiancee, eighteen years ago. Unfortunately, there had been complications and the uterus had been damaged during the process. The doctor said the hospital accepted full responsibility at that time. The young woman had been given counselling afterwards. The woman, who was also a doctor had left the area shortly afterwards and the hospital thought that she was now in the Midlands.

Henry knew of course who the doctor was. He was wondering what was coming next. He did not have long to wait. He heard all about the young Kumar's obsession with Professor Smythe, and how he had dumped his fiancee even though she was pregnant. Henry nodded and whispered in his weakened voice,

'I know this, Viv confessed once that she could not have children because of a botched abortion.'

'Doctor Kumar was murdered in the same way as the professor, Henry.' Miller looked at the man in the bed. 'The same type of knife was used. Her prints were found in the flat and were taken when the police were going over his flat for clues. However, as she was a regular visitor and fiancee of the young man, nothing had been made of this. Until, that is, the same prints were found in the professor's basement flat. According to hospital records, Doctor Mullen had stayed for six months at this address until she had found the house that she was now living in.'

There was silence in the room, broken only by the hospital sounds of trollies being wheeled and the footsteps of nurses going about their work. Susan cleared her throat and asked if the same doctor was responsible for the silent and then sinister phone calls? They affirmed that she was and added that the late Lizzie Dukes had been targeted as well. Several mobile phones had been found in her house as were tapes of all Henry's lectures and a key to the basement flat.

'Doctor Mullen is also lefthanded,' Jones said flatly.

'Why did I never notice that?' Henry asked.

'Probably because you are lefthanded yourself, and anyway, you would never have suspected someone so close and a professsional, like yourself,' offered Jones.

Henry face was shining with perspiration and he looked in distress. Jones rose and apologised for upsetting him and said that they would come back tomorrow. Henry shook his head emphatically.

'Tell me it all now. Please.'

Miller said the doctor was now in custody and was being very cooperative and not denying anything.

Lizzie had been lured to the flat, but it was to find the professor already dead. The knife was left deliberately, knowing the unsuspecting Lizzie would probably pick it up and leave her prints on it. But there was worse to come, they now suspected the doctor of being responsible for Lizzie's death and Henry's illness.

'But why?' asked Susan, 'She is so fond of those children, I thought that she just wanted to ensnare Henry.'

'She has admitted that she left strong tablets on her desk when she last saw Lizzie, knowing that the woman was desperate. She saw suicide as the best way out for her.'

Henry looked shocked and shook his head. 'No, I suspect now, having heard all this, that she thought the suicide would explain the murder and that the murder would go uninvestigated. She never thought for a moment that she would be suspected or found out.'

Jones rose to go and smiled at Henry. 'Sorry we had to intrude on the romance, doctor, we had to protect Susan, when we heard about the anonymous calls.'

Henry squeezed her hand and she looked down at him. 'It was the children she wanted,' he whispered, 'Poor Viv only wanted children, anybody's children, to love.'

'No doctor, first and foremost it was revenge. She was very patient, waiting for just the right moment to take her revenge on Smythe for nabbing her boyfriend and indirectly causing her inability to have children. Then along comes your poor wife. What a perfect opportunity for her. She now had a victim who would certainly be blamed for the murder and she thought she would get a readymade family too.'

'Why did she not commit the murder earlier, when she was living in the basement flat?' asked Henry.

'She was probably afraid to risk it, seeing as she would be the first one to be suspected.' Miller said.

'Oh! By the way, she would like to apologise to you doctor. She says it was nothing personal and that she really admires you. She knows you were not having an affair with Smythe. Seemingly she saw you throwing her out of your hotel bedroom once, while away at a conference. She says that you were the only doctor not taken in by that woman.'

'Is she remorseful about everything then?' asked Henry.

'With regard to Smythe, not at all! She says she'll die happy with what she did, sorry only for the upset caused to you and Lizzie. She feels guilty about that, alright, and hopes you will hide it from the children until they're both a lot older.' Jones shook his head in wonder.

The two detectives then left. Henry and Susan sat, still holding hands and silently thankful that it was now over, at last. Life beckoned and they at once thought of the Big Holiday promised the children.

Printed in Poland
by Amazon Fulfillment
Poland Sp. z o.o., Wrocław